COME MONDAY

COME MONDAY

CHIP BELL

WORD ASSOCIATION PUBLISHERS
www.wordassociation.com
1.800.827.7903

Copyright Registration No.: TXu 1-613-116
Effective: April 30, 2009

Printed in the United States of America.

ISBN: 978-1-59571-685-9

Library of Congress Control Number: 2011930249

Designed and published by

Word Association Publishers
205 Fifth Avenue
Tarentum, Pennsylvania 15084

www.wordassociation.com
1.800.827.7903

For my girls,
Linda, Jennifer, and Jessica

ACKNOWLEDGEMENTS

I would like to acknowledge Steve and Cindy Thompson for all their kindnesses in introducing me to Key West; Ed Morascyzk for always urging me to write a book someday; Bryan Pizzi for being a great law partner and better friend; Pat Denault, my sister, for taking time to review the manuscript; Eve, my secretary, for listening to me rattle on, having to put up with me making constant changes, and for spending so much time putting my words on to paper; Cynthia Nelson for having the patience, skill, and kindness to put forth such an effort into editing my manuscript and making it better than it ever was; Mike and Paula Langer for being the best friends a person could have; and finally, to my wife, Linda, for supporting me in pursuing yet anther dream.

SATURDAY

CHAPTER 1

It had to be the song. Jake Sullivan usually loved the drive from Miami to Key West, especially on a beautiful night. It had to be the song. There it was, coming from the radio. One of Jimmy Buffett's classics, "Come Monday, it'll be all right..." It was their song, he and his youngest daughter, Jessie. It had been ever since she was a little girl, and she still called him every Monday to make sure everything was "all right." But, she and her mother had been in Italy for almost a month on a foreign exchange program, and Jessie had been unable to call on a regular basis. He missed the sound of her voice. But, he had to admit, it wasn't only the song.

Traveling down the long line of islands that make up the Florida Keys at night gives a person plenty of time to think. During the daytime, you are swept away by the scenery stretching into the distance, the green Gulf of Mexico on one side and the blue Atlantic on the other, and if you time it just right, you can capture one of the most beautiful sunsets in the world as you head into the lower Keys en route to Key West. Jake knew he should be happy. The bag sitting on the seat beside him contained a check for $20,000—his fee for the successful salvage negotiation he had conducted with an insurance carrier for the total loss of a yacht owned by a rich Miami real estate dealer. His client had insisted on celebrating over dinner and drinks. Even though Jake tried to watch his consumption of Coronas, he knew he probably shouldn't be behind the wheel.

It was a warm night, and the top was down on his beloved BMW Z4 as he hit Florida City and began the trip down U.S. 1. He decided to go the old way and made the left at Old Card Sound Road, past the Mutineer Tavern, and headed down to the Monroe County tollbooth. The song had ended but he was still thinking about his daughter, which made him think about his past, and he felt himself sinking into that suffocating self-pity he hated so much. He wasn't a victim; he brought it all on himself.

Three years ago, he had been the chief prosecuting attorney in the Miami Office of the Justice Department. He had grown up in southwestern Pennsylvania in one of the steel towns that lined the rivers in that region. This was well before America stopped making things and the steel industry had moved to China. It was a great time to grow up. All those towns had been settled by immigrant families—Italian, German, Irish, Belgian, Polish, and others, to work in the steel, aluminum, tin, and glass factories. The towns were small, and even though there were distinct neighborhood differences based upon nationalities, everyone knew each other, and by high school graduation, you had friends whose families had come from all over the world for the benefits they believed America gave them. They worked hard, saved every penny they could, kept their small homes neat and clean, and sent their children to college. And those children came back to the towns and became teachers, doctors, lawyers, business owners, and leaders of the communities. It was a safe, wonderful place to grow up. Jake was always sad when he returned and saw the boarded up store fronts and litter, the grayness of everything, the faces that he no longer recognized; faces no longer filled with hope but full of despair. No one owned their homes anymore. Transients came and went, bringing with them the usual ruin, drugs, and crime. Those once prosperous little towns now sat like rusted links in a discarded chain.

Jake's father was a reader and he had always encouraged Jake to read. He grew up dreaming of palm trees and warm, sandy beaches, of pirates and the sailing ships of the Caribbean, and being top dog in the Miami Office had gotten him close to those dreams. He had a good life. He was good at what he did. He had a beautiful wife, Linda, and two beautiful daughters, Jennifer and Jessica.

It was hard to put a finger on why things started to go wrong. He had always considered himself a fair man, easy to get along with, well liked in the office, loved at home. But there was a part of him that couldn't walk away, a part of him that would tell an asshole he was an asshole, and that prevented him from following orders from someone he didn't respect or didn't like. Unfortunately, when the new President came into power, that someone, Benjamin Matthews, was appointed the new Attorney General and became his boss. To Jake, Matthews was a typical bureaucrat. He didn't understand the legal profession other than being a corporate lawyer for an investment firm in New York. He wasn't a trial lawyer. He didn't understand what had to be done to deal with criminals and crimes. He had no empathy and no concern for the victims of those crimes. All he cared about was the number of convictions, and how he looked on the cocktail circuit. Jake took an instant dislike to him and had to admit the feeling appeared to be mutual. Matthews was a frequent visitor to the Miami Office and always had something derogatory to say about the staff and the way the office was being run, although he wouldn't directly confront Jake, because he had yet another characteristic that Jake despised, cowardice. He had to laugh to himself, though. Here I am, the bastion of all that's good in the world, criticizing my former boss, and look at the paths our lives have taken.

Jake passed Alabama Jack's, the landmark restaurant of the entrance to the Florida Keys, passed through the tollbooth, and came to the stop sign marking the route that would take him to Key Largo and down through the Keys. His mind continued to wander back to what had been and what was. He knew at some point he had begun to drink too much. He knew it as it was happening, but in his mind, it was something he could control and really had no significance. Jake had only been a social drinker with the usual occasional lack of control in college or at special events. He didn't drink at home and drinking had never caused a problem in his married life until the first fight with Linda. He had come home late from the office again, she smelled it on him, and confronted him about it. In a manner typical of the drinker in denial, he became defensive and angry, and from that point on their family life was never the same. The hours spent at the office grew longer, as did the time spent in bars. Jake didn't consider himself an alcoholic. After all, he only drank beer. He used the rationalization of all beer drinkers—since he didn't like or didn't drink hard liquor, he wasn't an alcoholic. He always went to work. He always went home. He took care of his family. And he diligently took care of his cases. But, it was at work that everyone started to notice it. There were hushed whispers among his friends and colleagues. Glances were exchanged when he would ask "for just one more." And there was recrimination in the eyes of his wife and children. He put it off to the pressure of the job and believed that as things worked out and the job became easier, he would ease off and things would get back to normal. But the ultimate lie is the one you tell yourself. The job would never get easier . . . and the drinking wouldn't stop . . . and it all came to a head roughly three years ago.

He had the chance of a lifetime, a career opportunity that most people in his position only dream of. For almost a year, Miami had been under siege by a rapist and murderer that the media had dubbed the "South Beach Sadist," due to his proclivity to drop the abused corpses of his victims, whom he had raped and cut up, in various locations in South Beach. A young girl named Alaina Alvarez, a resident of the United States Virgin Islands, had been his tenth victim, and the interstate nature of the situation had put the case squarely in the jurisdiction of the federal government.

The FBI had been assisting the local authorities but took over the investigation, and this poor young girl had finally provided a clue that led to an arrest. The murder scene, her small apartment in Coral Gables, had been the usual horror show of blood and bondage, but Alaina had put up a fight. The killing ground appeared to be in the kitchen area and it was surmised by the FBI that the Sadist had come upon her while she was preparing dinner. During the course of the investigation, one of the agents was smart enough to notice some stir-fry in the skillet on the stove, but there was also stir-fry on the countertops and on the floor. It looked like those areas had been cleaned in a sweeping pattern. On a hunch that the food in the skillet had originally been on the floor and the countertop, the skillet was thoroughly examined and there it was. Something that this killer had avoided was leaving any trace of DNA, fibers, hair, or fingerprints at any of his crime scenes. But on the bottom of the skillet sitting on the stove was melted latex from the finger of a glove. It was always assumed that the killer had worn latex gloves. But if this poor girl had used the hot skillet in an attempt to defend herself, she may have swung at the killer and in warding it off with his hand, the latex covering his finger may have melted onto the heated surface, leaving the investigators with a means to recover a fingerprint from the inner portion of the glove.

A quick hit was obtained on the criminal database, showing that the fingerprint had a ninety percent positive match to one

Carlos Ortiz, a Mexican National living in Miami, who had a criminal record in Mexico and was suspected of various crimes here in the Miami area dealing with drug running and several unsolved murders. He had been arrested before, but there had been no witnesses willing to testify to his involvement in the murders. On the contrary, he brought forth a slew of witnesses who were willing to give him alibis for where he had been on "the night in question," to serve as "character witnesses," and to prove that the "Anglo" police were once again hounding an upright citizen of the Latino community. However, now they had the fingerprint and it was the key to the case. It was a definite match and it put Ortiz at the crime scene, and that was something that trumped all the alibis and other statements by the witnesses who were obviously scared to death to testify against Ortiz.

Jake and his staff worked long and hard preparing for trial. As he reviewed crime scene photos and coroner reports, Jake realized that he was dealing with a sociopath who would kill and cause pain without the slightest remorse. It was clear Ortiz needed to be put away for the rest of his life. When the latest victim's parents came to Miami from their home in the Virgin Islands to claim their daughter's body, they agreed to meet with Jake so he could get some background on their daughter. He could tell that their lives had been shattered forever. He promised them that he would put this madman away and that is exactly what he intended to do.

The investigation was difficult and time consuming and it didn't help matters any that Ben Matthews had taken a personal interest in the case. His presence irritated Jake for two reasons: First, the guy was there because it was a media event. He was there for the show. He was there to put his face before the cameras while Jake and his staff did all of the work. Second, he didn't know what he was doing. He constantly questioned decisions that were made and second-guessed everything. He wanted to know every last detail concerning the investigation, trial strategy, and what the chances were for conviction. Jake had to admit to himself that while those things pissed him off, the thing that really got to him was that he knew Matthews didn't give a damn about the parents he had met or the lives that had ended so horribly. He was only concerned about his own career and this case was just a rung up the ladder.

Jake had spent the days before trial establishing a trial schedule for witnesses and how the case would be presented. As was his custom, he worked from outline to outline narrowing his options as he created what he believed would be the best method of giving a great deal of evidence to the jury.

The day before trial, Jake went to the evidence locker and signed out the evidence box dealing with the case. He had the box opened by the evidence custodian and had it noted on the sign-in sheets to ensure there was no questioning the chain of custody. Jake could now review the evidence, which included photographs, investigative reports, lab reports, and most importantly, the lab analysis of the fingerprint obtained at the scene, which was secured in a sealed plastic bag.

When Jake was preparing his opening and closing statements, and determining which evidence he would use to lay out his initial case to a jury, he liked to have the evidence in his possession to determine whether he would show it to the jury in the opening, or wait and reveal it when the witness was on the stand. He always knew his case backwards and forwards, but it was that element of showmanship that any good trial attorney had to have that he obsessively honed on the day before the trial. He had to determine which photographs he would use and which he would not use, which portions of the investigative report he would stress, and which ones he would not. He had seen cases lost when someone had to dig around in a box trying to find something while the jury watched, making them question how involved that attorney truly was in the case he was presenting. Jake would review all the evidence and then place it back in the evidence box where he wanted it, knowing exactly where each item was. It would sit beside him at the counsel table where he could reach in, grab an item, and present it to the witness or to the jury through his opening and/ or closing remarks without missing a beat. After his strategizing was done, he would sign the evidence box back in to the evidence locker before the locker closed at 6:00 p.m. The day of the trial, one of the law clerks from the office would sign it out and bring it to the courtroom. As long as none of the sealed bags had been tampered with in any way, and the chain of custody had been documented and uncompromised, there could be no question of "tampering with evidence" raised by the defense.

Jake was known for his opening and closing arguments, and these were going to be the best ones of his career because Carlos Ortiz was not going to be on the streets to harm anyone else; he would make sure of that. He would present an opening to the jury so persuasive they would want to convict without even hearing the rest of the case. He was just finalizing everything when the call came in.

It was Matthews. He looked at his watch; it was just after 5:30. Jake gritted his teeth and got ready for another irritating exchange

"Jake, are you all ready for tomorrow?"

"Yes sir, I am. Everything is ready to go."

"You know Jake, I don't need to tell you this is a big case."

For your career, Jake thought. "Yes sir, I know it is."

"This guy is a sick son of a bitch and I want him off the streets. Do you understand me?"

"Sir, you do realize that's why we're working so hard on this case? To make sure that's exactly what occurs—that this guy gets put away forever."

"I know Jake, I know. Look, I know I've been on your back a lot, but you know I've seen those photos and read the statements of some of the parents and I can only imagine how they feel. This guy's a monster and I don't want anybody else being butchered."

Christ, thought Jake. Was this guy putting him on or was he sincere? "Sir, all I can tell you is that I'm ready to go and I'll do my best."

Matthews continued the conversation, making sure Jake understood what he thought were the key points of the case. Jake sat and listened, rubbing his eyes and trying not to pick a fight. Finally, Matthews seemed satisfied that he had given Jake sufficient instruction on how he wanted the case presented.

"Jake, I want you to know that I have complete confidence in you, all right? Well, I'll let you get to it. Good luck."

"Thank you, sir," Jake said, and hung up. Jake sat and stared at the phone and suddenly felt weary. Was he wrong about Matthews? Was he too critical? Did Matthews care? Was he just trying to make sure that his staff was doing their best on such an important case? Maybe, but Jake had his doubts. There was something about Matthews that no matter how much he expressed concerns for others, you felt his only real concern was for himself.

Jake glanced at his watch. "Goddamnit," he exclaimed as he slammed his hand on the desk. It was past 6:00 o'clock. The evidence room was now closed for the night. Jake finished boxing up all the evidence as precisely as he wanted it and put the lid on the box. He had two options. He could leave the evidence in the office and have the clerk bring it over in the morning, or he could take it with him and bring it to court himself. He opted for the latter. The evidence was in his custody and keeping it in his presence ensured an uncompromised chain of custody. He wasn't going to risk the defense implying that the evidence could have been tampered with while left unattended overnight. It also gave him another opportunity to rehearse his performance at home later that evening. He knew he wouldn't sleep, he never did before trial. His mind was always running with the openings, the closings, issues that might come up, points he had to make, and having the evidence available to him could help him should he come up with a question or problem that he hadn't already thought through.

Jake left the office and headed for the parking garage. When he got to his car, he opened the trunk and put the evidence box and his briefcase inside. Before leaving, he called home to see what was going on with Linda and Jessie. His oldest daughter Jenny was away at college and Jessie was a sophomore in high school. Linda had taken a job teaching at one of the elementary schools outside of Miami. The phone at home rang until the answering machine came on. Linda was probably at the PTA meeting or doing something involving her kids and Jessie was probably out with her friends, hopefully doing a little studying.

Jake hung up and pulled out of the garage ready to make the right turn toward home when the old demon pulled at him one more time. He made a left, and didn't stop until he pulled up at the curb in front of Mac's. The place was pretty quiet, even for seven on a Tuesday. Only a couple of people were at the bar, none of whom Jake knew, and he took his seat. Mac, an immigrant to the warm climes of Miami from Scotland, immediately came over.

"So, counselor, what will it be tonight? Another late one at the office, I take it."

"Yeah, Mac, big case tomorrow. Just give me one Corona, then I'm heading home."

Jake caught the knowing look Mac gave him.

After one too many beers, Jake exited the saloon and walked to his car. When he went to open the driver's side door, he saw that the window had been broken. Looking inside the car, he breathed a sigh of relief, as it did not appear that anything had been taken or damaged. Cursing softly under his breath, anticipating the hassle of having the window fixed, filling out the necessary reports for his government owned vehicle—all of which would constitute a genuine pain in the ass—Jake sat heavily behind the wheel. It was only when Jake looked down to the ignition to insert his key and his eyes traveled to the trunk release that a feeling of dread swept over him. He popped the release, got out of the car, went to the back, and slowly lifted the trunk lid.

Looking back, it was at that moment that Jake had that pang— that sudden stab of fear and knowing that comes with true disaster. When you know that however something ends, it's going to end badly. Both the evidence box and his briefcase were gone, and with them the evidence that squarely placed Carlos Ortiz at the scene of the horrific crime, which would lead to his conviction and life sentence.

Jake paced all night trying to come up with arguments that he could use to have the court grant a stay, to get a continuance to see if the evidence could be recovered. But in his heart, he knew it wasn't going to work. The evidence was gone. The chain of custody was broken. Even if the evidence was recovered, anyone could now claim it had been tampered with. The best evidence rule required the originals be submitted as evidence, and the original was gone.

The next morning in court, Jake made all his arguments. It was like sleepwalking. He was there but his mind was somewhere else. He could remember hearing the defense counsel object. He remembered all the terminology: best evidence rule, chain of custody, motion to suppress, request for dismissal, and the denial of all of his motions. The judge was clear. The only evidence linking Ortiz to the crime was the fingerprint evidence, and the fingerprint evidence was gone. Without that connection, the prosecution could not make a case. When the judge finally dismissed the case with prejudice, Jake knew his career was over.

Sitting here now, while driving to Key West, the images that still burned in his brain were the eyes that met his when he walked out of that courtroom. One set radiated pure evil and contempt as Ortiz walked to freedom. And the others, the eyes of parents who had depended upon him and whom he had failed, radiated despair.

The rest of the events had come in rapid succession. Matthews had flown to Miami and clearly enjoyed publicly castigating him for his failure to properly maintain the evidence and for allowing a serial killer to go back on the streets, although his most joyous moment was firing Jake and dismissing him from the Justice Department. The recriminations, even among friends, began immediately. The primary accusation being that his drinking was the cause of his problems, and secondarily, that he had become obsessed with the Ortiz case—the obsession and drinking feeding off each other, making him lose perspective and judgment. But all Jake could remember were the eyes. He saw them when he was awake, and he saw them when he was asleep, and he saw them in the bottom of the glass, which he began to see even more often than before. If he wasn't sitting in a bar, he was sitting at home, usually in a darkened room, trying to make the eyes go away, but they never would.

Jake was wallowing in guilt and self-pity. His law career was over and as far as he was concerned, his life as he knew it was over. Linda and the girls tried so hard to show their support, to show him that they didn't blame him for what had happened, that it wasn't his fault, and that they were there for him. And in return, he pushed them away because he knew it *was* his fault that a killer was still loose on the streets of Miami, and it *was* his fault that he was losing everything that he cared about. He lashed out at those that tried to help him, including Linda and the girls, and finally, Linda had had enough. She was kind enough to make up an excuse that she had to go back home because her dad was ill and needed her. Since Jessie was going to enroll in college soon, they went to look at schools in the northeast section of the country. Jake knew that she was leaving him and he didn't argue with her. He let her go. Jenny had finished college, gotten married, was a teacher, and had settled near her mom in the Pittsburgh area. Both girls still called him weekly. Hell, Linda called him at least twice a month and he knew that the connection was not fully severed. There was still something there, still something to salvage, but every time he thought about trying, his past failure rose up in front of him like a wall that he couldn't scale. Weeks passed into months and months passed into years. And here he was, alone, back on the road to Key West.

CHAPTER 2

Key West, Cayo Hueso, Bone Island, Margaritaville—the end of the road. The home of pirates, poets, artists, musicians, and lost souls, who in an attempt to find something else through necessity, compulsion, or desperation, wind up here.

Even with the onslaught of tourism, the island still held its charm. It seems that it had seen everything come and go. At one point in the 19th Century, it was the richest city per capita in the United States based upon its main industry: wrecking—salvage from boats wrecked on the many reefs around Key West would be claimed by those bold enough to go out and take them, leading to fortunes being amassed. Reminders of those days were still here in the beautiful Victorian style homes that dotted Old Town. With the arrival of the U.S. Navy, the building of lighthouses had put an end to the wrecking industry and the inhabitants of the island had to rely on shrimping and other forms of fishing. When economic depression hit, Key West was battered unmercifully, and in the 1930s it became the poorest town in the United States. Jake had talked to people who had moved to Key West in the 1960s and the early 1970s and claimed homes as squatters because of all the vacant properties. It became a counterculture haven. The main port of call for misfits, drug runners, poets, authors, singers, and anyone who thought they could be the next Hemingway or Tennessee Williams.

After he had lost everything and Linda had left, Jake had been sitting in Mac's one night when Steve Townsend sat down on the stool next to him. Townsend had been one of Jake's witnesses in a maritime fraud case he had prosecuted involving the resale of damaged watercraft, wherein the culprits had claimed the boats were totally destroyed, received insurance payments, and then went into the resale business. Steve had bought one, and realizing he had been had, had gone to the federal authorities and broke open the case. Jake and Steve had become friends after he had testified and Jake would occasionally go fishing on one of Steve's charter boats that he kept on Islamorada, halfway down the Keys.

"What brings you to Miami?" Jake said.

"Actually, I was looking for you."

"Well, here I am."

Steve looked at Jake. His eyes were darkened, obviously from lack of sleep. He had the stubble of a day's growth of beard and his clothes were disheveled.

"Jake, I know what happened. Are you all right?"

Jake smiled. "As much as I can be."

At that moment, the bartender came over.

"Mac, give me another Corona and see what my friend here wants."

"I'll have one of those, too," said Steve. "Jake, I'm here 'cause I need your help."

"What kind of help?"

"I need a good lawyer."

"I don't know if you've heard the whole story, but ah . . . I'm out of the lawyer business."

"You still have a license, don't you?"

"Yeah, for all the good that it does me"

"Well, I want to hire you as my lawyer."

"What is this Steve, a charity case?"

"Look Jake, I don't know everything you've gone through. I don't know everything you're going through. But I know that when you prosecuted that insurance fraud case you were one hell of an attorney. I've got a problem and I need a good attorney. I know you. I trust you. And I want to hire you. It's as simple as that. I'm willing to pay you a percentage of what you recover for me on one condition."

"What's the condition?"

"That you clean up your act, clean up yourself, and you slow down on the Corona."

Jake stared long and hard at Steve. "You're asking me to give up an awful lot. What's the percentage?"

"I think the going rate in Key West is 20%."

"What the hell are you talking about, Steve?"

"Look, here's the deal. One of my boats went down in a heavy rainstorm in the Keys. It was in good shape. There was nothing wrong with it, but I'm insured through Maritime Agency. They won't pay me because they said that my pumps weren't working properly and if they had been, the ship wouldn't have gone down, and since it's my fault, they're not going to pay. Jake, I just checked those pumps. They were working perfectly. It was just a bad storm and there was nothing we could do. We got everybody off. We tried to save her, but we couldn't. She started to take on water and she went down. Pumps can only handle so much."

"What's the value?"

"$120,000.00."

Even in his condition, Jake could do the math pretty easily—$24,000.

"Look, Jake, you don't have to decide right now. You've got my number. Think about it. Call me or come down to Islamorada if you want to do it, but let me know soon. I've got to get somebody on this. Thanks for the beer."

And with that, Steve was gone.

Jake sat there and thought about things. The house in Miami was up for sale, so he had to find a new place to live. He had always liked the Keys. Maybe this money would give him a new start, or maybe he was just kidding himself. Maybe he was just better here sitting at Mac's. He was still thinking when Mac came over.

"Hey, Jake, couldn't help but overhear the conversation. Take the guy's offer."

"When did you become my advisor?"

"Hey. I'm your bartender. That gives me the right to be your advisor. Take the job." Mac, who had been in the amateur golden gloves couldn't help himself. "Look, the fight ain't over. You did good in the first couple of rounds. You got knocked down in the fifth. It's a ten-round fight. Get back on your feet and go beat the guy."

Jake got up and paid his tab. "That's what you don't understand, Mac. I lost the fight. It was a knockout. It's over."

"Hey, there's always a rematch. Go take the job."

After that, things just seemed to work out. Jake got a buyer for the house in Miami and it was wrapped up within a week. He now had to look for a new place to live. Sitting there with boxes of stuff to be shipped to Linda and the girls, and stuff he was going to keep, alone at home, he kept thinking about what Mac had said. What the hell, he thought, and picked up the phone and called Steve Townsend.

It had taken less than a month. Jake had always been a good negotiator. He had gotten in contact with one of the experts he had used in the insurance fraud case and had him examine Steve's boat and gotten a report that the pumps were not at fault, as Steve had said. That and the threat of a claim for bad faith punitive damages had won over the insurance company and they paid the full value of Steve's boat. With his portion of the monies, Jake had made the move to the island. He found an upstairs apartment on Whitehead Street above a shop selling tourist bric-a-brac. Given the boating industry in the Keys, he began a new career negotiating settlements with the various insurance carriers up and down the islands representing individuals whose boats had been lost or damaged.

Within a year, he had been able to buy the shop below him, turn it into a law office, and hire two people: his secretary, Eva Badoux, a "conch", someone who had actually been born in Key West and had descended from the original settlers of Key West, rather than one of those who had immigrated to the island, and Hector Sanchez, a Cuban immigrant who was a jack of all trades—sometimes a driver, sometimes a handyman, sometimes a gofer—a good, honest man who worked hard at whatever he was asked to do, even though he constantly mumbled about being put upon by his boss. It was Jake's belief that Eva had come to know the business as well as he did and he left the day-to-day running of the office to her. As often happens between an employer and employee who are dedicated to the same purpose, in this case, client satisfaction, their thought process seemed to mesh. Also, Eva was very good at reminding Jake of his foibles, was not shy about correcting the errors she saw being made, and offering her opinion when she thought something might be done in better fashion.

Jake was just passing through Marathon when he looked at his watch and realized it was 3:00 a.m., on what was now Saturday. He also realized he was very tired—too much reflection and too much beer. He was about to exit Marathon onto the Seven-Mile Bridge, that part of U.S. 1 connecting the middle Keys with the lower Keys that ended at Bahia Honda State Park, and decided when he got there he would pull in and rest for a couple of hours. Accidents on U.S. 1 were notorious and he didn't want to become one of the statistics read about in the Key West Citizen. Although the park was technically "closed," access was possible, and there was plenty of room to pull off, lock the doors, and hopefully fall asleep without dreaming about the past.

He was about five miles out of Marathon when he spotted the vehicle on the right-hand side of the road. As soon as it came into his headlights, he realized it was a State Police cruiser. Jake immediately went through the charade that all drivers who had been drinking go through. He sat upright in his seat, clenched both hands on the steering wheel, and shifted his body weight to appear more erect, more conscious, and more sober. He made sure his seat belt was adjusted properly and passed the State Police car without looking in its direction, all the while reducing his speed. Looking back in the mirror, he saw no lights and heard no sirens, and he immediately slumped back into his seat.

It was at this moment the thought struck Jake that the State Police car might be staking out the entrance to the park. It was a known late-night meeting place for undesirables, and he had the thought that perhaps he should just keep going. But, the fear of an accident was greater, and he came up with a plan. He would pass the northern entrance of the park, cross the bridge, coast off to the side of the road, turn off his lights, make a U-turn, and *enter* the park via the park exit. The police officer would have a clear view of his lights passing the entrance and receding out of view, and Jake would be able to get the catnap he so desperately needed.

Jake slowly passed the entrance to the park, saw no activity, crossed the bridge, cut his lights, and pulled over to the side of the road. Although there were clouds passing in front of the moon, visibility was still good, and Jake had no difficulty making a U-turn, coming back across the bridge, and entering what was normally the exit near the Buttonwood Camping Area.

Jake had been to the campsite many times over the years and had taken the girls there on a couple of occasions when they had come to visit. He decided he would go to the southern end of the island farthest away from the police officer posted northbound. He passed the boat ramp and the main marina and went over to the picnic shelters on the other side. Pulling into a spot under a tree, he turned off the engine, and closed his eyes, hoping sleep would come and memories would fade.

CHAPTER 3

Jake wasn't sure what woke him—an unfamiliar sound, some sense of something out of the ordinary, or he had merely rested enough—but he popped awake as he usually did, which was wide-awake with his senses alert. He looked at his watch. It was 4:30 a.m., and he had slept for approximately an hour and a half. He felt rested, but his legs were cramped and his back was sore and he decided he needed to stretch. He got out of the car, and with a sense of caution he didn't really understand, quietly closed the car door. He decided to walk eastward along the southern edge of the marina, toward the overlook and boat tours and rental area.

The moon was bright, casting shadows that gave an eerie look to the railroad trestle above him. What the dreams of one man can accomplish, he thought. Henry Flagler, son of a poor New York minister, became a partner of Rockefeller and Standard Oil, and became a real estate promoter and railroad developer who opened Florida to the masses. He was credited with founding Palm Beach. In 1905 he decided that his Florida East Coast Railway should extend from Biscayne Bay to Key West. At the turn of the century, Key West was Florida's most populous city and it was the United States' closest deep-water port to the proposed Panama Canal. Flagler sensed there was money to be made in the additional trade with Cuba and Latin America, as well as what could be obtained through the new canal and, by 1912, the Florida Overseas Railroad was completed to Key West. The glory days of the steam railroads were dying when the Great Hurricane of 1935 hit the Florida Keys, destroying a great deal of the railroad. After that, its right-of-way was sold to the State of Florida and the Overseas Highway was built upon some of its bridge tresses that still stand today. The unused portions like the section looming above Jake are now fishing piers and some are designated historical landmarks. Right then, Jake heard a noise that seemed out of place. It sounded like muffled talking, and then he saw a light. For a brief second, he froze. Had the officer entered the park? What was his blood alcohol? He could see it now, "Local Lawyer Arrested for Drunken Driving." As thoughts raced through his mind, he forced himself to calm down. No need to be so edgy. He would explain that he was simply driving home from Miami after a late night of work, had gotten tired, and had decided to pull off and go to sleep. Sounded like the actions of a sane man and not a drunken driver. It might actually get him points with the local police.

Again, something cautioned him, and he decided to alter his route and turn south. He turned to go around the Sand and Sea Nature Center, through the picnic area, and proceed up along the Atlantic, to the area where he thought he had seen and heard whatever it was.

As Jake approached the Sand and Sea Center, he hugged the wall of the building closely and looked around the southeast corner, staying in the shadows as best he could. On the other side of the building there was a large light illuminating the parking area, and he did not want to step out into that light until he had had a look at what might be up ahead. Hugging the building, he looked to his left and froze. He stood there staring at a sight he couldn't quite believe. Was his mind playing tricks on him? He flattened against the wall, his heart pounding, and almost let out an audible gasp. Sneaking his head around the corner to see, he confirmed what he could not believe.

Two hundred feet in front of him in the side parking area were four cars: two black SUVs that appeared to be Escalades, and two other SUVs that appeared to be, to Jake's experienced eye, government issued vehicles. A group of men, all armed, formed a circle in the midst of the vehicles. Some were dressed in black suits, and some in street clothes, but they all were staring at the open trunk of one of the SUVs illuminated by the headlights of one of the other cars. And there in clear view of Jake Sullivan, in deep and animated discussion, was Benjamin Matthews, Attorney General of the United States, and the man Jake knew to be the South Beach Sadist, Carlos Ortiz.

CHAPTER 4

The scene before Jake's eyes couldn't have been any more surreal. Here was the personification of evil he knew to be a killer, over whose escape from justice he had lost everything, in some type of transaction with the man who had fired him over that very escape. The man standing before him wasn't simply Benjamin Matthews, Attorney General of the United States, but Benjamin Matthews, who next summer was reputedly going to receive the Republican nomination for President of the United States.

Even Jake had to give the man credit. He had been able to do what no one else had done: win the war on drugs. In conjunction with the Mexican and Columbian governments, he had successfully destroyed the Colombian and Mexican drug cartels. One by one, their leaders had been eliminated, and their members dispersed. The cartels had been a blight on American society for years, fueling drug use in the United States and making fortunes for the perpetrators in Colombia and Mexico. Matthews had been able to eliminate the Medellin Drug Cartel in Colombia, which had been operated by Juan Ochoa and Pablo Escobar in the 1970s and 1980s and was more recently run by Daniel Rendon, known as "Don Mario." However, the biggest problem for Matthews had been the rise of the drug cartels in Mexico. But, over time he had successfully destroyed the Juarez Cartel, led by Carrillo Leyva, and "La Familia," having just recently captured Rafael Gonzales, one of the leaders of La Familia, with the other main leader known only as "El Carnicero" missing and presumed dead. The Colombian and Mexican governments were able to regain control of their countries, and they entered into a treaty with the United States allowing U.S. intervention when necessary to ensure that the flow of drugs did not start again. Right now, he was enormously popular with the American people and his nomination, and ultimately his election, was almost assured. So, why was he here at 4:30 in the morning on a remote stretch of the Florida Keys, meeting with a known murderer?

His cell phone had a camera, but would the flash give him away? Should he take the risk? If he held it out, out of the shadows in the light of the building with the light coming directly overhead, the flash might not be noticeable or even go off given the power of the lighting. It was worth a try.

Quietly, he took his cell phone out, opened it, made sure that the scene was within the lens framer, and holding his breath, pushed the button. He had been right. The flash did not go off. He quickly withdrew and checked to see that he had a reasonably good photograph of the scene and that the people involved were definitely identifiable. Now the question was, should he make his way back to his vehicle or stay put until this meeting was over and the participants left? He opted for the latter and stood there making no sound for another twenty minutes, until he heard the slam of car doors, and watched as all the vehicles moved up the Atlantic to catch the main road out of the park. Jake waited another ten minutes for good measure and then worked his way back to his vehicle, got in, and quietly shut the door. He sat there and thought about what he had seen. Nothing made much sense, but he knew who he had to talk to. It was time to go home so he could make arrangements to do just that later in the day.

Hearing no sounds coming from the direction where the meeting had taken place, or on the road above him, Jake started his car and again without lights, eased his way through the park to the southern exit, came out onto the road and seeing that there were no vehicles coming, entered the highway. Only after he was moving down the highway did he turn on his lights to continue his journey through the lower Keys to Key West.

He had only gone about ten miles when out of nowhere police lights appeared behind him and he was pulled over to the shoulder of the road. The police car passed him and pulled in front of him. He notice that this was a different vehicle from the one he had seen at the north end of the park. The number on the back of that vehicle had been clearly visible and was 114. The number on this vehicle was 238.

Jake sat, waiting for what was to come. As the officer approached, Jake rolled down his window and sat with both hands on the wheel. Jake was accustomed to being stopped. It seemed a fast sports car, especially a BMW, was fodder for motor vehicle tickets in southern Florida, especially while traveling down U.S. 1 in the early morning hours. He hoped that this would merely be another one of those occasions. Reminiscent of a TV sitcom, Jake asked, "Is there anything wrong officer," to which Officer Stephen Adams replied, as expected, "License and registration, please." Jake got his license from his wallet and registration from the glove compartment and handed them to the officer, who perused them for several minutes.

"It's a little late to be traveling the Keys, Mr. Sullivan. Where are you headed to? And where are you coming from?"

"I had an evening meeting in Miami and was driving home to Key West."

The officer seemed to think about that for a minute, then looked back up the highway. "You know, I was sitting off the road back there in some of the scrub, 'cause the only people we seem to get at this time of night are speeders and I'm trying to save people from ending up as a blotch on the road. I can see pretty far up the highway and I didn't see your lights until you were a couple miles away. Surely you weren't driving with your lights off, were you, sir?"

Jake wasn't sure what to say, given what he had seen this night, but figured the partial truth might be better than nothing. "To tell you the truth, officer, it's been a long ride and I needed a restroom so I pulled into the Bahia Honda Park and used the facilities there. Quick in, quick out. But, I had turned off my lights when I pulled in and I didn't realize they were off until I pulled out on the highway. That's when I turned them on and that's what you saw."

"How long ago were you in the park?"

"Couldn't have been more than five or ten minutes ago."

"When you saw the lights come on, I had just pulled out."

"How long did you say you were there?"

"Just long enough to use the facilities. Is there some kind of problem, officer?"

"Look sir, you have to understand, I'm sitting here on the edge of the road at 4:30 in the morning and I see headlights come on, on an already moving vehicle. Makes me curious. So, if you don't mind, I'll ask you the questions I think need to be asked."

"Sorry officer. I'm just tired. I want to get home. It's been a long day and a long night, and I don't really know what else I can tell you."

"Let me ask you this. We've been having a little trouble up at that park with people pulling in there and doing some things they shouldn't be doing. Did you see anything or anybody?"

Not really knowing what he saw, Jake decided discretion was called for. "No, as far as I could tell, I was the only person there. Like I said, I was in and out quickly.

"O.k. sir. Well listen, be careful on the rest of your way down to Key West. Make sure you keep your lights on and drive safely, o.k.?"

"I will, officer. Thanks." And with that, Jake pulled out, breathing a sigh of relief. He hadn't even been asked if he has been drinking.

A couple miles further down the road, though, he had the thought that it was odd that two State Highway Patrolman would be so close together on a stretch of the Overseas Highway at this time of night. But, the one had said they were having some trouble at the park and perhaps they were setting up some type of operation to try and stop whatever trouble there was. Immediately, he realized that made no sense, and a shiver ran up his spine. If a police officer was at the northern end of the park and there was a police officer at the southern end of the park, how did the group of vehicles he saw at that meeting get in and out without the police noticing them? There was only one conclusion. The police weren't there for some type of sting operation. They were there as guards to ensure that the meeting went privately with no one else entering the park while it was going on and making sure the participants had a safe exit. As Jake realized he had admitted his presence in that park, and what that might mean, two miles up the highway Officer Stephen Adams was already on the radio.

"Did you see anyone other than the group enter the park at any time?"

The reply came back, "No. As a matter of fact, the only car I saw tonight was a sports car, about 3:00 a.m., that drove on by."

"What did you say?"

"There was a sports car that drove by around 3:00 o'clock and I watched it go past the park."

"How do you know it went past?"

"'Cause I was up here near the north end where I could see it go past."

"What type of sports car was it?"

"One of those little BMWs."

"You sure?"

"Yeah, I'm sure."

"And he went past the park?"

"That's what I'm telling you."

"And you said the time was at 3:00 o'clock?"

"That's what I'm telling you."

"All right, thanks."

After clicking off the radio, he picked up the coded cell phone he had been given and pressed the button he had been told to press. A voice came on the other end.

"What?"

"We have a problem."

"What problem?"

Adams went through what had occurred.

"All right. We'll handle it. Who is this guy?"

Adams read what he had written down from the information on the license. "Guy's name is Jake Sullivan. Lives at 312 Whitehead Street, Key West."

"All right. Like I said, we'll take care of it. We'll call you if we need anything."

"Got it."

With that, they hung up.

In the back of a black SUV sat Attorney General Benjamin Matthews. The meeting had gone well, he thought. Another $20 million to go to the campaign coffers. His victory both for the nomination and the general election was practically assured. He would be able to outspend his opponent three to one and with his popularity almost twice as high as the incumbent President, he had no doubts he would soon be sitting in the Oval Office. Then this country could finally be turned in the direction it should be heading—away from the ridiculous policies of past presidents, including the current one, Jordan Fletcher, his former classmate at Yale and the person who had nominated him to be Attorney General of the United States. Fletcher was an old school liberal trying to save everyone, upholding the sacred virtues of America, but all he was really doing was eroding the power of the greatest country on Earth. Matthews knew better. He had seen all his life what worked, and that was power and money. Born into a rich Rhode Island society family, he had gone to all the best schools, including Phillips Exeter Academy, Yale, and Yale Law School. He had gotten a job at one of the top law firms on Wall Street, amassed a personal fortune, and made influential contacts. What Fletcher didn't understand was that you had to have a long-term plan, just like corporations do, and then stick to the plan and do whatever is necessary to make it work, including always making sure that you have proper funding to carry out the mission. And yes, some would say he was ruthless. Some would probably even call him a fascist. But Matthews understood that the weak had to be eliminated, obstacles that stood in the path had to be removed, failure was not an option, and that it was all right to make deals with the Devil as long as you were able to control the Devil. As long as the Devil was working *for you* to assist in the ultimate success of the mission. And here he was, so close. He knew Fletcher despised him. He knew that Fletcher now realized who he truly was, well, not who he *truly* was. That was something that no one would ever know. In the beginning, Fletcher had been easy to convince. He had started touting Fletcher for public office back at Yale, and he had to admit Fletcher had a knack with people. People trusted him, people liked him—things that Matthews really wasn't concerned about. Matthews knew that the ultimate way to control people was through fear and power, not popularity; popularity came and went. Power stayed and fear kept people in line.

Matthews had always been just at the edge of Fletcher's circle, just enough to give his opinion, just enough to lend a helping hand with money or a connection when it was needed as Fletcher embarked upon his political career. And when Matthews helped deliver the nomination and the election to Fletcher, it was then that Fletcher owed him, and it was then that Matthews asked to be appointed to the position he now held. It was easy to appeal to Fletcher; to sell him on being the President who would win the war on drugs. Matthews had a very convincing plan that he presented, and it was accepted. Of course, it wasn't the *real* plan. That was something Matthews had been working on for many years prior to Fletcher being elected, and all he needed was the power of the office to pull it off. And he had. Soon the necessity for meetings like tonight would end, and his dealings with murderous thugs like Ortiz would end. He was about to take America into a new era of being a multi-national conglomerate, controlling worldwide wealth and power, and then his phone rang.

"What is it?"

The voice on the other end quickly laid out the details that he had been given. "We have a problem, sir."

After listening to the whole story, Benjamin Matthews began to laugh.

"Sir?"

"It's nothing. It's just that this world truly is a small place and it's funny how your past keeps coming to meet your future."

"Sir?"

"Just forget it. I want this taken care of as quickly as possible. We can't have any loose ends."

"Understood, sir."

And with that, Attorney General Matthews closed his cell phone and sat back for the trip back to Miami. The only other thing coming out of his mouth was, "Well, well. Imagine that."

CHAPTER 5

The rest of the drive to Key West was uneventful. He finally made the right onto Roosevelt, headed into Old Town, and parked his car in front of his office/apartment on Whitehead. It was after 6:00 a.m. by the time he climbed the stairs to his apartment and closed the door behind him. He never noticed the black vehicle that had turned onto his street and passed his house several times before taking a position down the block. Given the hour and what the day was to hold, Jake decided to try and get as much sleep as he could. He took off his clothes, and lay down in bed. The thoughts of what had happened in the past several hours raced through his mind and it was difficult to go to sleep. He tried, but gave up around 8:00 a.m. He got up, showered, put on a T-shirt, shirt, and a pair of shorts, and went down the steps. He unlocked his bike from its stand, and began the ride over to Caroline Street to get breakfast at Pepe's, which was his custom. Fortunately, the restaurant wasn't crowded. It was a little too early for the tourists and there was only a smattering of regulars. He sat at the bar, and ordered the breakfast drink of choice at Pepe's, a mimosa with fresh-squeezed orange juice, along with his standard eggs over easy, home fries, and rye toast. After eating and exchanging some small talk with the staff, Jake paid his bill and decided to go for a ride. Although it was Saturday morning,

Eva would be in to go over the mail and plan the week ahead, but she usually didn't come in until 10:00 and it was only 9:30. He thought maybe a ride would clear his head and help him determine how he should proceed with the information he had.

It happened after he turned onto Simonton. Jake never saw the car, but he heard it. The sudden roar behind him made him jerk his head around just as a black SUV was almost on him. In a split second decision, he jumped from his bike onto the hood of a parked car, just as the vehicle ran over the bike. Nothing but wreckage came out the back end. By the time Jake rolled off the hood onto the sidewalk, the vehicle was gone. He pulled his handkerchief out of his back pocket and wiped the sweat off his face and neck. All he could think was that the car had been a little too similar to the vehicles he had seen the night before. As he retrieved the wreckage of his bike and began to walk back to Whitehead Street, the only thought that would come to him was, "Am I already in this mess and over my head without even trying?"

CHAPTER 6

It was just after 11:00 by the time Jake got back to his office. He stashed the wreckage of his bike underneath the steps leading to his apartment and came around to the front of the building and entered. As expected, Eva was sitting at her desk and Hector was there working on an overhead light fixture. Eva looked up as he came through the door.

"Jake, what in the world happened to you? You look like the wrong end of a long, late night."

"I wish," said Jake. "Some crazy son of a bitch just tried to run me over."

Eva, half-joking, said, "Maybe a disgruntled client?"

And, Hector, on his ladder, began to chuckle.

"Very funny," Jake said. "I'm serious. Someone actually tried to run me down just now."

Hector came down off the ladder. "Boss, are you sure? You know, there are a lot of crazy drivers in Key West these days, and nobody seems to see us folks who ride bikes all the time. It's getting more and more dangerous out there."

"I don't think this was an accident," Jake replied, as Eva got up from her desk and came to him.

"Jake, you got a big bruise on the side of your head. Let me do something about that."

"That must be where it bounced off the hood of the car I jumped on to get out of the way."

Eva reached up to touch the bruise and Jake pushed her hand aside. "I'm all right, I'm all right. Don't worry about it. Let's everybody get back to work."

Eva looked at Hector and said, "Well, it didn't take long for him to get back to the fun-loving, communicative Jake we all know and love so well."

Hector looked at her and said, "Maybe it *was* a client."

Meanwhile, Jake had retreated to his inner office and closed the door. He went to the sink, got a washcloth with cold water, and sat at his desk, holding the cold cloth to his head, thinking about what had happened, what he had seen the night before, and what he had to do. Jake had been a prosecutor long enough to sense when something wasn't right, and the events of last night were clearly not right, but he just couldn't make all the connections to prove what he was feeling in his gut.

Jake dropped the washcloth to the floor. As he always does when beginning a case, he got out a yellow pad and a pen and started to list what he knew and what he didn't know. After a half hour, he looked at what he had come up with:

    A.G.—Carlos Ortiz

    cops—park

    cops—me

    car—bike

On the right hand side, he looked at his notes that said:

    meeting?

    cops suspect?

    know who I am?

And the most chilling of all:

did someone try to kill me?

He dropped the pad on his desk and sat back in his chair watching the fan making lazy patterns on the ceiling. After thinking about everything, he could only come to one conclusion. The meeting he had witnessed was about something bad, and it was a meeting that no one else was supposed to have known about or witnessed. He had seen it, it was known that he had seen it, and because of that, someone was trying to kill him.

Jake went to the computer and dictated a summary of everything he knew and, along with the photo from his phone, burned three separate CDs. He was going to put one in his desk, one at home, and keep one on his person. Then he got out his Rolodex and looked up the number of an old friend in the FBI, Mike Lang.

Mike and he had become good friends after he had arrived in Miami. Mike was a hardnosed, no nonsense agent, honest to a fault, and dedicated, but without the blinders that a lot of agents have concerning the bureaucracy of the bureau. He had a common sense approach to things and a wry sense of humor that immediately endeared him to Jake. They got along well from the very beginning and had worked on many cases together. When everything fell apart in Jake's life, it was Mike who had come to him and asked if he could help in any way, and over a case of Corona, they had both got drunk and railed against the system, Benjamin Matthews, and the world in general. They had formed a bond that night and even created their own code. Mike had gotten upset that there were no limes for his Corona and Jake had given him the standard speech about putting fruit in beer and that the only proper way to drink Corona was NFL (No Fucking Lime). Probably because of the Corona, Mike had found this hysterical and during the course of their deliberations that night, they punctuated each of their conclusions by hollering "NFL." Jake had always appreciated that Mike had given him that one night to blame everybody else, even though they both knew where the fault truly lie.

Jake knew he could trust Mike, but this story was so beyond belief and involved such a prominent national figure that he wondered how Mike would react. He picked up the phone, and got through to the FBI switchboard in Miami. The switchboard operator indicated that Mr. Lang would not be in the office until Monday but did he wish to leave a message? Jake cursed silently, forgetting that it was Saturday, and absent some type of emergency, Mike wouldn't be in the office. He left his name and number and asked for a call back whenever possible. Realizing he also had Mike's home number, he called there but he had to leave a similar message. He put down the phone, sat back, and tried to think of how he was going to bring Mike onboard.

At that moment, there was a tap on the door and Eva stuck her head in. "Jake, I have those files you wanted to see. Do you feel up to it, or do you want to wait until Monday?"

"Na. I need to be doing something. Bring them in and I'll go through everything and then I'll leave you a tape with stuff to take care of on Monday."

Eva walked in and sat the files on the desk. "I've done everything else. Is there anything else you need before I go?"

"No, Eva. Thanks for coming in. Everything's good. I'll take care of it from here."

Eva started for the door and as she reached for the handle, turned. "Jake, should I be worried about you?"

Jake looked up with a slight smile on his face. Eva was one of those people who was so kind hearted. She always showed concern for everyone and he could see that concern in her eyes. "No, Eva. You and Hector were right. It's probably just some crazy driver that we get more and more of in Key West these days. I'm sure everything is fine."

Eva turned and walked out, but on the other side of the door she hesitated because she wasn't at all sure that everything was fine.

It took the rest of the afternoon for Jake to go through all the files; dictating letters to clients explaining the status of their cases, or threatening letters to insurance companies demanding compensation for those clients, and finishing off parts of investigations, or scheduling investigations for the near future. He had to admit that he had made himself a pretty good business here in Key West. One thing about being a lawyer, he thought, as long as you had your license there was always a job out there and there was always somebody who needed you.

By the time he finished and looked at the clock, it was almost 4:00 p.m., and he decided to call it a day. Jake just had to do one more thing. He took one of the discs he had made and slowly looked around the room, trying to determine a place where he could put it for safekeeping. "You're getting paranoid, Jake me boy," he thought. But, by the same token, he couldn't get what had happened out of his mind. And then he had it. Jake had a CD player in his office and a collection of CDs were on the shelf above it. He picked out one of his favorites, *Havana Daydreamin'*, by Jimmy Buffett, opened it, took out the CD, put the CD he had made inside, and put the CD case back where it had been. Standing back and looking at it, it appeared to be random and no different from any of the other CDs in the row. "Always hide something in plain sight," he thought. He then took the Buffet CD, put it into his carry bag, along with the two other CDs he had burned, and headed out to the front office.

As he entered the front office, he noticed that not only was Eva gone, but Hector, as well. Just as he was heading for the front door, it opened and Maria Calderone came in. Maria cleaned the office on the weekends, but she rarely came in until Sunday because she knew that Jake was usually in the office on Saturday. Maria seemed startled when she opened the door.

"Ah, Mr. Jake. I didn't expect you. I thought you'd be done for the day."

"Yeah, I had a little bit of work to do, Maria. How've you been?"

"Very good, very good."

"Everything o.k. Maria? You usually don't come in until Sunday, do you?"

"Oh, everything's fine Mr. Jake. I just have a nephew's birthday party in Miami tomorrow and my husband and I are going to head up right after I finish here."

"No problem, Maria. Everybody's gone for the day, including me. I'm on my way out, so the place is all yours."

As he was closing the door behind him, stepping out into the warm sun of a Key West afternoon, he thought of something, hesitated for a second, and then went back into the office. Ten minutes later, he was walking down Whitehead Street toward Duval, heading for the Chart Room, which had opened at 4:00 o'clock, as usual. The Chart Room was his favorite bar in Key West. It was just a small, six-stool little place made out of a motel room in the Pier House Resort. He liked it because it was quiet and off the normal tourist track, although not so much anymore, given the ability of Parrotheads to dig up everything there was to know about their hero, Jimmy Buffett. His references to this bar had caused it to become one of the shrines they visited on their pilgrimages to Key West. In the old days, it was the place where all the locals gathered, where politics was done, drug deals were made, criminal conspiracies were hatched, and God knows what else. Some of the regulars and old timers still came in and he liked to talk with them and listen to their stories. It was a dark place with photos covering the wall behind the bar of days present and past, pennants on the ceiling that looked like they'd been there for centuries, and usually the floor was covered with peanut shells from the barrel that was near the popcorn machine and free hot dogs. Thinking about the place, Jake thought he might have to reconsider its status—it was his favorite *inside* bar—his favorite *outside* bar currently being the Schooner Wharf, where you could sit out under the canopy and palm trees on a sunny day, listen to Mike McCloud sing, and watch the dogs get their very own scraps through the hole that had been cut in the kitchen wall.

The local ambiance of Key West was fast disappearing but there was still more here than most places in the world, and Jake loved every bit of it. The bar was quiet for a Saturday afternoon. He didn't recognize any regulars in attendance, only a bearded man whom Jake heard say had come down to Key West from West Virginia for a little bit of warmth and sunshine. Overhearing the guys references to Morgantown and the Mountaineers brought back memories of his own days growing up near Pittsburgh, and the bitter rivalries between his beloved Pitt Panthers and the Mountaineers of West Virginia University. He still followed Pitt, even though he hadn't been to a game in years. Tom, the bartender, knowing his habits, had a cold Corona, no lime, waiting on the bar by the time he took his seat.

"Well, Jake, what have you been doing on this beautiful Saturday here in paradise?"

"Just spent a little time at the office getting some work done."

"What's that knot on the side of your head? Someone refuse to pay their bill?"

Lawyer humor, thought Jake. Everybody loved it. Well, they couldn't say that lawyers didn't deserve everything they got, the way they've been practicing law the past twenty-five years or so. "Na. Just a little bicycle accident. Nothing major."

At that, the man from West Virginia looked his way and began a tale of why he didn't like bicycles and how dangerous they could be… Jake really wasn't in the mood for chitchat but he meant no harm and he answered accordingly and went along with the conversation for a while.

"You know, I don't drink that beer myself," the beard said. "I thought that everybody that drank it stuck one of those little pieces of fruit into the top of it."

Tom said, "Yeah, most drinkers drink it with a lime, but Jake goes NFL."

"NFL?" the beard asked.

"Pardon my language," Tom said, "but, No Fuckin Lime."

This brought a gale of laughter from Mr. Beard, but also seemed to be a fitting ending point for the conversation. Jake bought him a drink and was getting ready to leave when he looked out the side door and saw Annie Lewis coming down the path. Annie worked at the Recorder's Office in the Monroe County Courthouse and Jake had seen her there on many occasions over the last couple of years, and two weeks ago, had finally taken the opportunity to ask her out to dinner. She was divorced and left Missouri to come to the Keys and he, of course, had his story, as did everyone that came to this island. Jake often thought that was why it was so easy for people to meet each other here. They were all looking for something new and all running from something old, and everybody seemed to have the same take on things. Annie came in and slid onto the seat next to him.

Tom brought Annie her usual, a vodka and cranberry, and exchanged pleasantries.

"So, how have you been Jake? It's been a week since I last saw you."

"I know, Annie. Things have been busy. I've been back and forth to Miami on a case and just finished it up yesterday, as a matter of fact."

"What happened to your head?"

Tom chuckled behind the bar, knowing that the question might bring another saga from Mr. Beard from West Virginia. Annie looked at him, puzzled.

"Never mind. I just had a little bicycle accident. Everything's o.k."

Annie, as she did with most things, took Jake at his word and let it drop.

"So, how's everything at the courthouse?"

"The normal. Although I gotta tell ya, real estate in this town is selling back and forth faster than you can believe. All these problems with the real estate market haven't hit Key West yet. The prices keep going up. The people keep want'n to buy it."

"Well, it's everyone's dream to come to Key West and buy a little piece of paradise. So, I guess that's understandable.

"To think when I came here twenty years ago," Annie said, "the property I could have bought for so little . . . and what I could have sold it for now."

"Yeah, but people that came to Key West twenty years ago didn't think like that. That wasn't their purpose. They were here because they had reached the end of the line. They had to cross water to go any further. Some of them did. A lot of them couldn't. But you know what, the place is warm, it has palm trees, it has a feel about it that makes you want to be here. You gotta love a place where people applaud sunset every night (referring to the sunset celebration on Mallory Square where the local population and, of course, now tourists, turned out to watch the sun set into the Gulf)."

"I suppose you're right," said Annie. "I wasn't even sure I was coming here when I left Missouri and somehow I just ended up here. I guess you're right about why I stayed."

They had a couple more drinks and chatted and Jake said, "Look, it's almost 6:00 o'clock. Do you want to go get something to eat?"

"Yeah, sure. I don't have any plans," said Annie.

"How 'bout A and B for some fish?"

"Fine with me."

Jake left a tip for Tom and they said their goodbyes. Mr. Beard, had departed for some other sites of Key West some time earlier, so they left the bar empty as they went out the door and headed for Front Street.

Walking toward the restored Key West Seaport, Annie looked at Jake. "Last time I saw you, your daughter had gone away for a while. Is she still away?"

"Yeah. She's in Italy for a month as a foreign exchange student. She should be home tomorrow or the next day. She hasn't been able to call, and I miss her usual Monday phone calls."

"And your other daughter, it's Jen, isn't it?"

"Oh, Jen still calls every week. I talked to her on Wednesday. Everything's going fine with her and her husband. She's helping out with the cheerleaders. They're in the middle of ending football season, starting basketball season, so she's busy, too."

"You're lucky Jake to have two children who love you so much."

Jake knew that Annie's marriage had been childless and he didn't want to push the issue, but he had to agree. "Yeah, they're good kids, but I sometimes just feel that I've lost something with each of them and I don't know how to get it back."

"You will Jake," said Annie, "you will."

Annie and Jake decided to make a night of it. They both had the broiled seafood platter at A and B and decided to have a nightcap at the Schooner Wharf. The bar was crowded, as usual, but Annie got a seat at the bar and Jake stood while they had their drinks and talked with friends. Jake's troubles passed from his mind due to the quantities of alcohol being consumed and being back in what now constituted his world. It was a beautiful night in Key West and his worries faded as the night went on.

SUNDAY

CHAPTER 7

By the time Jake and Annie left, it was after midnight. As they came out on the wooden planking and walked up the steps past the icehouse (which was the worst kept secret in the world as being Jimmy Buffett's recording studio, Shrimp Boat Sound) they came to the intersection for Green Street. Annie lived down on Eaton.

Looking up at Jake, she asked, "You want to come over to my place?"

It had been a good night with Annie, free from worry for a while, and he enjoyed her company, but something stopped Jake from accepting her invitation and he wasn't quite sure what. Something was just not quite right.

"Annie, I'm still a little sore from this bike accident. Would you mind if I took a rain check tonight?"

There was an obvious show of disappointment in Annie's eyes, but only fleeting. She smiled at him and said, "Sure. Not a problem. You can walk a girl home, though?"

Jake gave her his arm. "Madam, the age of chivalry is not dead." After a brief hug and kiss at her door, Jake took Eaton to Duval, stopping and looking back over his shoulder as he did so. His thoughts were running rampant. He tried to focus on the situation he was in—the danger of it, the unanswered questions, how it was all going to work out—and even with all that had happened, that wasn't the central thought in his mind. He kept coming back to Annie's invitation and why he hadn't accepted it. Deep inside, he knew why. He was still in love with Linda. He had loved Linda from the moment he met her and he still loved her. He loved his girls and the life they had, and he missed them horribly. He had made a new life for himself in Key West, but it wasn't the life he wanted. It was a life that had grown from the seed of his own mistakes and the flowers it bore, fragrant or not, were not entirely to his liking. He was like a rat in a maze, wanting to get to the end of one thing, but back to the beginning of another and not knowing how to do either. He was deep in thought and had turned onto Duval Street when the phone rang. The caller ID indicated it was the FBI Offices in Washington and he knew he was about to speak to Mike Lang.

"Jake, it's Mike."

"Thanks for getting back to me. Did you get the package?"

"Yeah, I got it. Pretty clever, sending me a CD with your cleaning lady. Why the cloak and dagger?"

"Mike, did you see what was on the CD?"

"Yeah, I did."

"Mike, there's more. Someone tried to kill me yesterday morning."

"What? What happened?"

Jake went through the whole encounter with the speeding black sedan.

"Are you sure it wasn't just some crazy Key West driver?"

"Why does everyone think I'm making this shit up? Why does everyone think it was just an accident? I'm telling you—I saw something I wasn't supposed to see and because of it, somebody out there is trying to kill me."

"Jake, Jake, take it easy."

"Look, I'm telling you, there's something dirty going on here and Matthews is in it up to his neck."

"Jake, slow down. Look, before you go accusing the Attorney General, and probably future President of the United States, of trying to kill you, let me tell you some of the things I've found out."

"What?"

"Matthews summoned me to a late night meeting in D.C. I found the CD from your cleaning lady in my office when I stopped by to pick up some papers before catching my flight, and I brought it with me. Matthews said he had some information he had to give me, it was bad news, but he was giving it to me because it involved a friend of mine. Jake, that friend was you."

"What the hell is he talking about?"

"Just listen to me. Look Jake, I'm sorry to tell you this but I'm afraid there's going to be a grand jury indictment coming out. You've been named as a person of interest in an investigation into insurance fraud in the Florida Keys."

"That's bullshit. I used to prosecute insurance fraud cases. I'm an attorney handling salvage claims for boat owners."

"Jake, I'm telling ya. They have sworn affidavits from individuals who say you are involved in this, how the whole operation started, and how it's been going on. They have a guy that says you paid him money over the years to bring you business, and that you've doctored insurance claims, and now Matthews is coming after you."

"Who's the son of a bitch that signed affidavits against me?"

"One Stephen Townsend and his wife Cindy."

Jake couldn't believe what he was hearing. "Steve Townsend's one of my good friends. He was the guy I originally helped that made me move to Key West and start this practice."

"Look, Townsend's affidavit says that he came to you because he knew you were a disgraced attorney, just fired from the prosecutor's office in Miami. He figured you were an easy mark to get involved in something shady and you went for this hook, line, and sinker and you've been running this scam with him ever since. He and his wife both signed these documents under oath and they're going to be presented to a grand jury next week, and based upon what I see in this affidavit, the grand jury is going to bring back an indictment and Matthews is going to send me down to personally arrest your ass."

"Mike, you know me. This is bullshit! I'm not involved in any of this!"

"Jake, look, you're my friend, but I'm telling you what we've got here. If an indictment is returned against you, I'm gonna have to come get you."

"Look Mike, what about the CD? Did you see it?"

"Yeah, I saw it. I even brought it up with Matthews."

"What? You gave it to him?"

"No, I didn't give it to him. I still have it. But I told him that there was an unsubstantiated report that he and his men were seen meeting with a person of ill repute early Saturday morning in the Florida Keys."

"I bet that shook him up."

"Not really. He was very matter of fact about it. He said he was meeting with an informant who he was using to gain information to catch the last member of the cartels in Mexico, El Carnicero—that this guy had been his informant for years and that they had met on numerous occasions at this location out of safety concerns for him and the informant. He said he had trip schedules, mileage indicators, and that any of his men were willing to give sworn statements to the fact at any time, if this was of some concern. Jake, the

CD doesn't show anything. It shows a meeting with Ortiz, who he alleges is his informant giving him valuable information in the war against drugs. Jesus Christ Jake, the guy's going to be President of the United States. What do you want me to do with this? There's nothing there."

Jake sat down on a low wall.

"Jake, are you there?"

"Yeah, I'm here. Mike I'm going to tell you something. I know this guy's dirty. I know what I saw and I know what happened to me. This son of a bitch ruined my life once and it's not going to happen again. This time I'm fight'n back."

"Jake, don't make threats. I'm still with the FBI."

"Mike, you've got to make a decision—whether you're going to be with the FBI or you're going to be my friend. You do what you got to do, but I'm gonna do what I got to do."

And with that, Jake slammed the phone shut and turned it off. Jake sat there, trying to collect his thoughts. Things hadn't made sense before and they made less sense now. He knew Steve and Cindy Townsend as well as he knew anyone in Key West. They were his friends and they were good people. And documents they allegedly signed obviously weren't true, so why would they do it, if they did it at all? Signatures could be forged. But why them? How were they being used? Jake couldn't believe that they were part of all this, not voluntarily. But what about involuntarily? And then there was Mike, the one person he had looked to, the one person he thought was going to help him. Thinking about the evidence before him though, Jake couldn't fault him. He had been given sworn affidavits and other documentation from the Attorney General of the United States and all Jake had to go on was a meeting that Matthews easily explained away, and a crushed bicycle under his steps. What if I'm wrong, thought Jake? What if Matthews was meeting with this informant? What if that's what Ortiz was? But Jake knew he was a killer. But how could Jake argue that when the charges against Ortiz had been dropped because of Jake's mistakes? Did it all smack of revenge on Jake's part? Is that how it would be played out? Jake stood up and looked around. Duval Street was one of the greatest streets in the world. It was a place where the nightlife never seemed to end and people from all over the world mingled. There were characters galore, bars a plenty, shops, and it gave you a feeling that you were some place special. But Jake didn't feel special tonight. Unless something happened, unless he found proof to support what he knew to be true, the one person he trusted most in the world to help him would be on his way to Key West, not to help him . . . but to arrest him.

Suddenly very weary, Jake made his way to his apartment on Whitehead Street and went up the steps. His head ached from all the thinking, maybe a little from the accident, maybe a little from the Corona. All he wanted was his bed and a good night's sleep. He unlocked the door and looking at the key in the lock, remembered that there was an extra set of keys hidden in the pouch on his bike. Maybe it was a little paranoid, but he decided to go get the extra set out of an abundance of caution. He was halfway down the steps when the world went white.

CHAPTER 8

Most bombs have two common elements: a trigger and a timer. Sometimes the bomb is set to be activated just by the trigger and it will go off immediately, as soon as the trigger is engaged, but if you need to make sure the thing you want to destroy has moved into the destructive path of the bomb, then you use a delay switch. Jake unlocking the door was the trigger. The ten-second delay saved his life. The bomber had wanted Jake to enter that apartment and gave him ten seconds to do so—the same ten seconds that allowed Jake to get halfway down the stairs before it detonated.

Jake came down hard on the ground. Ears ringing from the concussion of the blast, momentarily blinded by light, bruised and cut from the wooden debris falling around him, lying on his belly, almost unconscious, he heard sounds and saw shapes through a haze, everything tilted at an odd angle. Gradually, he was able to focus and he was able to observe two things. One, there was a shard of wood sticking out of his left forearm, blood coming out of the opening it had made in his arm. Two, there were a pair of black shoes attached to black pants moving rapidly towards him. Even though it hurt like hell, he elevated his head and let his eyes travel up the black pants, but they didn't get very high when he realized there was a gun with a silencer held out in front of the pants and shoes, moving in on him at a dead run. Adrenaline is a wonderful thing; it has saved many a life. Jake felt it surge through his body. He wasn't sure if Black Pants and Shoes had seen him raise his head, but now he lay very still, eyes cracked just enough to see. His face was in the crook of his arm and he hoped Black Pants would check to see if he was already dead before he put a bullet in his brain.

Luck was with him. Black Pants moved his foot towards Jake to nudge him over so he could see his face and just as his foot came near Jake's arm, Jake grabbed the pant leg, yanked and rolled at the same time, pulling Black Pants' legs out from under him and laying him on his back. His left arm hurt like hell but Jake was fighting for his life. He ignored the pain, sprung up, and immediately was on top of Black Pants wrestling for the gun. "Pfft" went past his head as Black Pants got off a shot. Aside from the heat, it didn't appear there was any damage. It didn't take Jake long to realize he was overmatched. Black Pants was a professional and he began by elbowing Jake everywhere he could, but Jake knew that he had to hold onto the gun. With the last bit of strength he could muster, he pulled and they both rolled. It was a losing proposition. Black Pants was getting the upper hand and Jake knew he couldn't hold on much longer. The cut had taken the strength out of his left arm. Jake had one chance and he took it. Bracing himself for the pain that was going to come, he released his right hand from Black Pants' wrist and yanked the wooden shard out of his forearm, letting out a scream as he did so. The scream was enough. For a brief second, Black Pants stopped fighting, and in that second, Jake drove the shard of wood into Black Pants' throat and rolled over on top of him. Black Pants squirmed for a while but then stopped. Jake slowly got off the body, knowing full well he was dead.

Looking back at what had been his apartment and office, Jake realized that the bottom three steps of the flight that had gone to his apartment were still there and he sat down, heavily. What had been a beautiful Saturday night had turned into an ugly Sunday morning. Now, he had no doubt that all the notes on his yellow pad pointed to one thing. People were trying to kill him and he had to figure out what to do.

Jake's reverie didn't last long. He heard the loud roar of an engine and saw headlights coming down Whitehead. No police sirens or lights, though, and he knew in his gut that it was Black Pants' friends. Wrapping his handkerchief around his wound, he knew he had to move quickly. Christ, he thought, the keys to the car were upstairs and he wasn't sure there was much "upstairs" left, or if the keys still existed. Then he remembered the other pair in the desk. Jake hesitated until he was sure the lights of the car would catch his movement. He ran through the hole where the door to his office used to be. He hoped was that whoever was in that car would follow. He ran through the debris to the inner office. His desk had been knocked aside but it appeared to be in one piece and he yanked at the bottom drawer. It was stuck. He heard the slam of car doors. He didn't have long. Jake pulled and pulled and finally with one last burst of strength, the drawer came open and he fumbled inside until his hand wrapped around the keys. Jake crouched down, hoping he wouldn't be seen, and crawled to the bathroom. His luck was still with him. The bathroom window was blown out, so he climbed through and dropped as quietly as he could to the ground on the side of the building. He listened briefly until he heard footsteps and people thrashing around inside what had been the outer office. Slowly, he moved around the build-ing. He couldn't see anyone in the car and there was no one out front. His Z4 was parked five cars down on the left hand side of the street. Staying in the shadows, he moved toward the car and quietly opened the door, and got in. Before starting the engine, he looked in the rearview mirror and saw two of Black Pants' friends coming out of what had been his office. He turned the key, the ignition caught instantly, and he threw it into gear and sped off down Whitehead. He heard a "pling" as a shot hit his trunk. He kept looking in his rearview mirror and saw the lights jump away from the curb and head in his direction. "Christ," thought Jake, "a car chase—like in the movies—that's just what I need."

Annie had made herself a cup of tea when she had gotten home and was sitting in her living room, thinking about Jake. She liked him, but saw no future for them. Jake clearly loved his daughters and she admired that in him. The troubling thing was that he also clearly still loved his wife. But still, he was here and so was she. Damn it, Annie thought, why do I always complicate my life like this? Just then, she heard a rap on her door. Her heart skipped. Maybe Jake had changed his mind. Annie opened the door to greet him when her hello turned into a muffled scream as a gloved hand covered her mouth and pushed her back into her apartment, the door closing behind them.

CHAPTER 9

Jake cursed his luck. He had had no time to pick up his bag and, in fact, didn't even know where it had landed. He didn't have the disc, he didn't have his phone, and had no way of contacting Mike or anyone else. All he had was the gun taken from his would-be killer. Jake had never had much use for guns, even though he had received an expert ranking in the Army. But then he was only shooting at targets, not people, and he seriously doubted his skills in a shoot-out with people obviously trained to kill.

His only hope of getting out of this alive was evasion. He had to lose the car behind him. He only hoped he knew the streets better than Black Pants' friends, but where to go, and who could he trust? He remembered the Highway Patrol Officers and wasn't sure who was trying to kill him or who all was involved.

Quickly, he cut his lights and yanked the wheel to the left on Petronia. Keeping his lights off, he then made a right onto Shavers Lane and then a left on Olivia. When he made the next left onto Simonton, he turned his lights back on and drove the whole way down to Green, where he cut his lights again and pulled in along the side of Sloppy Joe's. He jumped out of the car, and headed for Duval. Even at this time of night, Duval was packed with people. He could mix with the crowd until he could get hold of another vehicle. He hadn't seen lights behind him since he turned onto Shavers Lane and he hoped he had lost his pursuers, but if they had followed him, he hoped this plan would work.

Ahead of him, were a bunch of young people crossing the street heading in the direction of The Hog's Breath and he walked alongside the crowd, hoping to mix in and stay out of sight. Moving down Duval, he tried to stay within crowds of people, looking for his pursuers as he went. So far, so good.

He was about to cross Fleming, hoping that there would still be a large crowd hovering around Margaritaville, when he saw what he needed. A taxi was sitting on the corner near Fleming and didn't appear to have a passenger. He went over to the cabbie and got in the back.

"Listen. I have two hundred dollars. I need you to drive me up to the marina on Cudjoe Key."

"Hell, pal. For two hundred bucks, I'll drive you to Miami."

"O.k. Let's go."

The driver pulled out and made a right onto Duval.

"Do me a favor, will you? Circle back around and come up on Green Street near Sloppy Joe's."

The driver looked in his rearview mirror and Jake could see questioning in his eyes. Jake also knew he must look like a vagrant at best, but then he saw the driver's attitude shift from questioning to acceptance. What the hell, the driver thought, It's Key West. Don't ask any questions, just take the money and go.

Coming up on Green Street, Jake slid down into the seat so that he was barely able to see out the windows. The two men in black were standing by his car in a heated discussion, obviously trying to decide what they should do.

As they were turning the corner back onto Duval, Jake was able to see the man on his side of the car as he passed. He recognized him instantly. He wasn't wearing a beard, but there was no question in Jake's mind that the man hunting him down on Duval Street had been sitting on a bar stool earlier that day in the Chart Room, claiming to be a tourist from West Virginia. Jake had figured that if they had been able to follow him and find the car, they would think he had set out on Duval Street to mix with the crowds and would follow.

"Head for Cudjoe. I've seen enough," Jake said.

And the cabbie made the turn on Roosevelt and headed up U.S. 1.

CHAPTER 10

Thirty minutes later Jake was knocking on the door of a house that sat on Cudjoe Bay. The drive out of Key West had been uneventful, but his injured arm had been uncomfortable. The bleeding had stopped, but it was a relief to let it rest a bit. As they hit Cudjoe Bay Key and passed the missile tracking station that had been set up during the Cuban Missile Crisis in 1962, they turned at mile marker 20 to go back towards the marina. Away from immediate danger, his mind wandered. Always a curious thing, Jake thought, the use of mile markers instead of street addresses in the Keys. Mile marker 0 is at the end of Fleming Street in Key West and mile marker 127 is just south of Florida City, and references to points in between are based upon their distance from Key West.

Jake had the cabbie stop at the house he was looking for on Cudjoe Bay. It was a well-kept one-story block building and Jake could see a boathouse past the driveway, down on the bay. There was a nightlight on but it didn't appear that anyone was moving about. At this time of night, Jake figured he was going to wake somebody up.

Jake knocked and was about to knock again when the door opened and there, behind the screen door, stood Tom Carrington in T-shirt and shorts, obviously having been aroused from his sleep, and Jake couldn't help but notice that his hand held, what appeared to be, a gun of substantial size.

"Jake, what the hell are you doing here at this time of night?"

"Tom, I need your help. I need somebody I can trust."

"What are you talk'n about?"

"Just let me in and I'll explain everything to you."

"Jake, you look like hell. You're not in trouble with the law, are you?"

Jake couldn't help but laugh. "Tom, just let me tell you my story and you decide."

Tom hesitated a moment and then unlocked the screen door and beckoned Jake in.

Tom Carrington was the former Sheriff of Monroe County. He had lost in the last election a couple of years ago. There were rumors of graft and misuse of funds, but nothing was ever proven. Jake had met Tom at the Chart Room and they had become friends. Tom had set up a charter business taking fishermen out onto the flats to catch the bonefish that live in the shallows of the Keys, and had taken Jake out a couple of times. Jake had always found Tom to be no nonsense, and regardless of the rumors, he seemed to Jake to be a man of some integrity. At this point, Jake needed help and he was hedging his bets. Even though Matthews tentacles obviously reached into Key West, Jake figured they wouldn't reach to a Sheriff who had *lost* an election.

"Sit down, Jake. You look like you could use a beer."

"In the worst way, Tom, in the worst way."

Tom went over to a refrigerator, took out a bottle of Key West Lager, opened it, and handed it to Jake.

"Here you go."

"So, what the hell is going on?"

"Tom, I'm gonna tell you to begin with, you may not believe this story."

Tom looked at Jake. "Try me."

And so Jake did. A half hour later, the story had been told. Tom had sat and listened and didn't interrupt. Jake told him almost everything. Tom got up and walked around, shaking his head and paced back and forth for several minutes.

"Jake, I gotta tell ya. It sounds crazy, but I don't think anybody could make this shit up. Benjamin Matthews, the guy that's going to be the next President of the United States, somehow involved with a serial killer?"

"I know, I know," said Jake. "It doesn't seem to make any sense, but it's true."

"I believe you—I just can't figure it out. You think these guys that tried to kill you work for him, right?"

"As best I can tell."

"Let me see that gun a minute. Maybe it'll tell me something."

Jake realized he still had the silenced weapon in his waistband. He took it out and gave it to Tom. He winced as he moved his arm.

"It sure isn't government issue. It's a Beretta with a silencer. The feds usually use Glocks, but then again, if they're doing what you say they're doing, they won't want anything traced back to them. It looks like the serial number has been filed off.

"Tom, look. I don't want to get you involved in this, but I didn't know where else to go. Can I use your phone? I need to call a friend of mine who may be able to help me with this."

"Yeah, sure. Before you do that, though, let me make some calls. I still got some contacts around the Keys and up in Miami. Maybe I can find something out and give you a little bit more information to give to your buddy."

"All right. Thanks Tom. I appreciate it."

"You just sit here, have another beer and relax."

Jake started to get up to get another beer, and thought better of it. He couldn't sit and started walking around the room. It was a modestly furnished place. As far as he knew, Tom didn't have any family and he didn't see any pictures to prove otherwise. There were some awards, some citations, and then something caught his eye. He crossed the room to a bookcase and what he saw made his blood run cold. There *was* a picture in the room. The *only* picture in the room. It was a picture of Tom in full uniform, receiving some type of citation, and the citation was being presented to him by Benjamin Matthews.

Jake moved to the room where Tom had gone and he heard Tom in a muffled voice still talking on the phone. As quietly as he could, he started making his way to the front door, his senses telling him that something wasn't right, the picture confirming it. He had his hand on the doorknob when the voice came from behind him.

"Don't Jake. Don't open the door. Turn around."

Jake looked at Tom and saw the Beretta he had given him, pointed directly at his midsection. Jake's shoulders slumped.

"So, you too, huh?"

"Jake, I'm sorry. You know, the money I was able to skim while I was Sheriff didn't pay for much of a lifestyle, and retirement isn't worth a crap. When Matthews gave me that citation, we had a little talk. He gave me his spiel about the drug war and how he was winning it but needed help in the Keys. He needed someone to be his eyes and ears, but he wanted it in an unofficial capacity, so the son of a bitch rigged the election so I would lose. He's the one that put out the rumors about the skimm'n and the corruption and all that other shit. So, now I get my salary plus a sweetener, I get to go fishing, and all I've got to do is provide information. One of his boys had called me earlier and told me they were looking for you. And how sweet is this—all I had to do was get out of bed, and here you are."

"But, Tom, you know this guy's dirty. There's something going on here."

"Dirty? You know what's dirty? The Goddamn Cubans and other bastards that moved into the Keys and turned this place into drug central. You know how much shit goes up and down these islands, into Miami, from there to God knows where? You know how many kids get hooked on that crap? Matthews is doing what he has to do. He's the only guy trying to stop this stuff. It's destroying this place. It's destroying this country. And if I can help him, I'm glad to do it. I know, I know—his ways might not be the cleanest. He might not go by the book, but he's getting the job done. He's getting rid of the scum bags dealing this shit."

"Tom, you know they're going to kill me."

"Hey Jake, I don't know what you did. I don't know what you're involved in. Matthews's guys said you're dirty, that you're involved in all this. All I'm doing is turning you over to the Feds for them to deal with you, and then I'm out of it. Now, sit down! They'll be here soon."

"Guess I picked the wrong guy to trust."

"Hey Jake, don't forget, you're the guy that fucked up in Miami. You put that scumbag back on the street. I don't know what he's doing dealing with Matthews but as far as I'm concerned, if he's dealing with him, then Matthews has him under control and Matthews is using him for something. And all I know is they don't want you fucking this up again. Now sit down and shut up!"

Jake realized it didn't matter what he said. There was no hope of convincing Tom. There were millions of Americans out there that felt just like he did, which is why Benjamin Matthews was about to become the next President of the United States. And, of course, it didn't hurt any that Tom's patriotic fervor was fueled by greed in the payoffs that Matthews gave him.

Jake sat back down in the chair, defeated. Tom leaned against the wall across from him, leveling the gun at him. It seemed like an eternity, but about twenty minutes later Jake heard the sound of car engines, and then the door swung open.

One agent walked in. And then another one came in, and Jake just shook his head. Different clothes, no beard. It was clearly the guy from West Virginia he had seen in the Chart Room, and that he had last seen on Duval Street next to his abandoned car. And then the next guy came in. It was all Jake could do to keep from leaping out of the chair, regardless of the guns pointed at him, because as the door closed behind him, there stood Benjamin Matthews, Attorney General of the United States.

"Jake. Long time no see." Matthews then turned to Carrington. "Tom, you did a nice job—appreciate all the help. I think we're done now."

And with that, the former Beard from West Virginia turned and shot Carrington right between the eyes. The back of his head exploded against the wall and plaques and trophies came down with him as he slid to the floor. And Jake knew he was about to die.

CHAPTER 11

"Jake, I gotta tell ya. You've been expending a lot of Federal resources. You had my boys running everywhere trying to get a hold of you." Matthews walked around the room as he talked, his hands stuffed in his trench coat pockets, taking in the room but not looking directly at Jake. "So, how have things been going for you, Jake? I hear you've got a nice practice down in Key West. Not quite an ambulance chaser, but more like a boat chaser."

"Fuck you, Matthews," said Jake.

"Jake, Jake, that's no way to talk. Not after all we've been through together. You know Jake, when I first met you, I thought you'd fit right into my plan. But then I realized you have that moral streak in you, that follow the book, do what's right, don't trample on anyone's rights approach and I knew it just wasn't going to work."

"Obviously, you don't share the same sentiments."

Matthews came close to him, and looked him in the face. "I do what I have to do to get things done. This country was being turned into a shit hole by people outside our borders bringing their dope into this country and I've put an end to it. You see, Jake, before I was Attorney General, I was a businessman. I worked for corporations, and I learned a lot working for them. You can't win the war on drugs. There's too much money in it. There's too many people getting paid. So, you've got to have a business model. You've got to consolidate and you've got to control. And you've got to have somebody that knows what the other guy's doing. It was simple— brilliant, but simple. I had to find my guy in Colombia or Mexico, make him see my point of view, and then eliminate everyone else. Like I said, the distribution of drugs is never going to go away— too much money. But it can be controlled. And by controlling it, you can reduce it, and you can direct it where it needs to go, and keep it away from where you don't want it to be. And that's what we did."

"So, you're tell'n me that you now control the drug trafficking from Colombia and Mexico to the United States?"

"Exactly. You got it on the first try, Jake. Very good."

Jake thought about the implications of what Matthews had said, and then he realized something. He looked up at Matthews. "El Carnicero."

Matthews now had his hands behind his back and was rocking on his feet, smiling.

"You're work'n with El Carnicero. You had him eliminate all the other members of the cartels in Colombia and Mexico. You had him disappear from the face of the earth, but he's your connection to the dealers."

Matthews started laughing. "Always the quick study, Jake. Always the quick study." He turned to one of his men and said, "Bring him in." One of Matthews's men went outside and Jake let out an audible gasp when the door opened and in walked Carlos Ortiz, the South Beach Sadist.

"Jake, you know Mr. Ortiz. But allow me to introduce him to you by his other name . . . El Carnicero."

"Matthews, you're telling me that your connection is this goddamn killer?"

Them both standing there, smiling at him, was more than Jake could take. He lunged from the chair in the direction of Matthews and Ortiz, but one of Matthews's men caught him as soon as he began to move. As the gun came down on the back of his neck and everything started to go dark, all Jake saw was Ortiz's eyes—the same look he had seen three years before.

CHAPTER 12

A bucket of cold water woke Jake with a start. Shaking out the cobwebs, trying to orient himself to where he was, was like coming out of a bad dream, but then he saw Matthews and Ortiz and everything came rushing back. Jake realized he was sitting in a chair, his hands handcuffed behind him, and his wounded left arm was throbbing. He heard the sound of the water. Looking around, he realized he was at Carrington's boathouse. Matthews began to talk.

"Jake, you always were a hothead. Just sit and relax. We'll get this over with quickly."

"Get what over with? You going to kill me?"

"Jake, of course I'm going to kill you. I can't have you running around calling the FBI and telling stories about me and my associates."

Jake looked at him curiously.

"Yeah, Jake. I know you called Lang. Why do you think I called him up to D.C.? I had to discredit you. Given your past history, it wasn't that hard to do. See Jake, we got word that you were down here in the Keys scamming insurance companies and we got an affidavit from one of your clients to that effect."

Jake slowly shook his head. "Steve Townsend."

"Yeah, Mr. Townsend didn't want to do it at first, but after a while he became very cooperative and signed the necessary papers."

"What did you do to him?"

"Well, he had an accident in his boat out at sea. He and his wife, both. I'm afraid that they're not going to be around anymore."

"You miserable bastard."

"Jake, haven't you learned yet? You've got to control the evidence in these things."

At that, Ortiz burst into laughter and Jake finally knew. "It was you. It was you three years ago. It was all a setup, wasn't it?"

"Jake, you were getting too close. You used a lot of my time. I had to be in Miami all the time monitoring your actions, and then you got that goddamn lucky break that put you right on the trail of my associate here. So, what could I do? I could have killed you then, but it would have seemed out of place. I could have threatened you, but like I said before, you're the moral type. You wouldn't have gone for threats. So, the only thing left was to ruin you. So, I made sure you had the evidence the night before trial. Jake, you are a creature of habit. You were drinking too much. You had some problems. So, it was easy to follow you. As soon as you made the left out of the parking garage, we knew you were going to Mac's. While you were inside, one of my boys broke the window, took the evidence box and the briefcase, no more case, no more Jake. And Mr. Ortiz was free to do what I needed him to do."

"Matthews, what the hell is wrong with you? He's a psychopathic killer."

At this, Ortiz stood up and started walking toward Jake.

"Carlos, not yet. Jake, there's no need for name-calling. I realize that now and again Carlos's proclivities lead him to wander off the reservation, but you see, I needed someone who could kill without any concern. I had to eliminate the competition in Colombia and Mexico and I learned very quickly that Carlos here was my man, that he could destroy whole families if he had to. That didn't bother him. He was exactly what I needed."

"You take Spanish in high school, Jake? No? So you don't know what El Carnicero means? Let me translate . . . 'the butcher.' Need I say more? You know, Jake, I realize there were some innocent people hurt. We had to look the other way. It was for the greater good."

"You moralizing son of a bitch. You're no better than he is."

Matthews's face grew red. His eyes began to bulge and he lowered himself until he was only inches away from Jake's face. "How dare you! How dare you compare me with anyone! I'm the only person that did anything about the problem destroying my country. It was a war, Jake. There are civilian casualties in a war. Do you realize that I'm on the edge of being able to run this country, to eliminate all the weaklings, all the bleeding hearts, all the intellectuals, all those who want to give free passes to the weak, to the needy, to those that are destroying the very fabric of America? And Jake, the beauty is most of those people will kill themselves. We control the supply lines, the major source of drugs coming to this country, and we can direct them where we need them to be, and we can wipe out the users, and we can use the money to do great things to restore this country, to make it what it once was. Don't you DARE compare me to anyone!"

He was mad. There was no question. He was completely insane. Jake was dead anyway and he could only make one final comment; he spit directly into the face of Attorney General Benjamin Matthews. Matthews recoiled, and Jake thought he was going to hit him, but just like that, Matthews regained his composure, took out a handkerchief, and wiped off his face. He looked back at Jake and smiled.

"By the way, Jake. We got all the discs. I knew you had sent one to Lang. I'll have him turn that over to me and it will be destroyed, but I already explained it away with him, so it's not a problem. Hiding one with the other CDs—that didn't work. We picked up your backpack when you left, so we got the copy you made. And quite frankly, Jake, the CD wouldn't have worked very well. You see, everybody at Justice knew I had a secret informant who was giving me information and helping me win the war on drugs. And my meeting in the Keys that night with Mr. Ortiz here was merely to gain information. My agents here will testify that we did it on a monthly basis, that he was our main conduit in trying to find El Carnicero, the one remaining drug dealer. And his information has been instrumental in allowing the Colombian and Mexican government to hunt down the other members of the cartels."

Matthews looked over at Carlos. "Carlos, you might even get a citation." And Ortiz sat there and smiled. Jake's head sagged. He knew that Matthews was right. All this, and he really hadn't proved anything. He knew Mike doubted the evidence. And with the means at his disposal, Matthews could fabricate a story that completely explained away what he was doing at Bahia Honda that night. Jake was going to die and Matthews wasn't going to be stopped and it had all been for nothing.

Matthews must have sensed the despair in Jake's face. He chuckled and said, "Jake, don't feel bad. It's just another example of you not being very good with evidence. All right, Carlos . . . guys . . . leave us alone for a second. I've got to talk to Jake here, man to man."

After they went outside, Matthews turned to Jake. "Jake, I've got to apologize to you. I have a slight problem here that I have to take care of and, unfortunately, it involves you."

"Matthews, I don't want to hear any more of your bullshit. Just kill me and get it over with."

"Now, see Jake. That's the point. Based upon our past working relationship and our mutual affection, I'd like to have my men put a bullet in your head and be done with it. But like I said, I've got a problem. See, Carlos has become a liability, and sooner or later he's gonna make another mistake and there's gonna be someone else like you out there that's going to figure out who he is and he's gonna get taken into custody, and I can't quite say that I trust Carlos 100%. He might feel compelled to save his own skin by giving up mine. Fortunately, I've been able to make contacts in the Colombian and Mexican governments where there are people who think like I do and are willing to assist me in the marketing scheme I've developed. So, I really don't need Carlos anymore. And you know, I'm afraid Carlos has had a long, healthy hate for you, Jake. You know, you almost put him out of business, and he didn't take kindly to that. I think he's been harboring a grudge against you for years and I think, as a matter of fact, he's tried to kill you a couple of times, now. We've found someone in Key West who actually witnessed that bicycle accident you had and the license plate number on that car is traceable to our friend, Mr. Ortiz. Also, I wouldn't be surprised if the investigation by the ATF agents relative to that bombing that occurred tonight didn't show Mr. Ortiz's fingerprints at your house and office. And then, of course, the other unspeakable thing he did tonight. I mean, you know, it's just horrible. I mean, he couldn't be satisfied just killing you."

Jake suddenly became alert. "What are you talking about? Matthews, you bastard, what's he done?"

"Well, I've gotten word that, unfortunately, there's been another murder, very similar to those that occurred in South Beach, tonight in Key West. Another young lady. I think her name was Lewis . . . yes, Annie Lewis."

Jake struggled with handcuffs behind his back, struggling with all his might to get out of that chair, screaming at Matthews, "You murdering son of a bitch! I'll kill you if it's the last thing I do! I'll kill you!"

"Jake. Don't get mad at me. I didn't do it. It was Carlos. He's uncontrollable. That's what I'm trying to tell you. But, the only thing that makes sense is for him to kill you. And you've seen his work. It's going to be painful, Jake, and I'm sorry for that. But it's the way it has to be."

Jake was completely defeated. His thoughts went to Annie. What she must have gone through before she met a horrible death.

Finally, Matthews came closer. "Jake, look, I'm sorry about the girl. And I'm sorry about you. But I want you to know that when Ortiz is finished with you, I'm leaving one of my guys here and he's gonna take care of Ortiz. So this will be done, and it won't happen again."

All Jake could do was stare. Matthews backed off a little and cocked his head. "Jake, if I didn't know better, I'd think that was hatred in your eyes. Well, let's get this over with. I have other things I have to do. Jake . . . wish it could have worked out differently." And with that, he was out the door.

A few minutes later an agent came in and stood to Jake's left, and then Ortiz came in, still smiling. Looking at Jake with that horrifying smile on his lips Ortiz slowly took off his leather belt and produced a handle from his pocket, which with one quick movement, opened into a straight razor. Ortiz approached him, razor in hand.

"You know my name. That was one good lookin' lady you had. We had a good time together. Man, I was in every hole she had, and she was begging me for it, and then when I cut her, she bled like a pig."

Jake wanted to reach out and grab hold of his throat and squeeze the life out of him. He had had a thought after Matthews left and he knew it was his only hope. He struggled to keep his composure and stared back at Ortiz. "You know Ortiz, I knew when I worked on your case that you were stupid, but I didn't know that you were this stupid."

Ortiz started to turn around and then just like that, lashed out with the razor, cutting Jake across the chest. Jake grimaced in pain, clenched his fists, and looked up at Ortiz.

"I'm stupid, huh? You're the one that's going to bleed, mother fucker."

"Yeah. But when I'm dead, you're gonna be dead, too, mother fucker." Jake saw it in his eyes. He had him. It was now or never. "What do you think this asshole is still here for? I'm in a chair with handcuffs and you've got a razor. You think we need somebody on guard duty?"

"Shut up," said the agent and moved toward Jake.

"Yo, man—you stay right there!"

"Think about it Ortiz. You're a loose end. I caught you. Someone else is gonna catch you. You think Matthews wants that to happen?"

"I said shut up!" and the agent hit Jake on the side of the head with his Beretta. Jake slumped to the side, fighting to keep consciousness.

Ortiz turned and shouted at the agent, "I told you to back off! This is my show!"

"Then get it over with and quit talking."

"Man, you shut the fuck up!"

"Don't listen to him Ortiz." Jake pressed on. "You're not getting out of here alive. This guy's only here to take you out."

Ortiz had walked over to his coat and had his back to Jake. "You know, Mr. Prosecutor, you talk way too much. The only thing I want to hear coming out of your mouth from now on is screams." And with that, Ortiz turned around, but the razor was no longer in his hand. Instead, it was a revolver, which he raised at the agent and fired. The agent must have sensed what Ortiz was going to do because in the same instant, his own weapon was out and shots came back in reply. Jake tipped the chair to his right, falling hard on his right side, the right side of his head striking the floor, and lay there.

It had gone quiet. All that remained was the smell of gunpowder and cordite and a wisp of smoke heading toward the lights and the ceiling fans in the boathouse. Jake inched around on his side, the chair moving with him. The agent was slumped over, not moving, and he couldn't see Ortiz. He listened carefully, and he could hear groans coming from the direction Ortiz had been. Jake slowly began to move his arms up the back of the chair. It was excruciating. His left arm still throbbed from where the piece of wood had been stuck in it, and his wrists were raw from being cut by the handcuffs, but he inched them slowly up the back of the chair, pushing off with his feet against the wall, until finally he was free of the chair. Still groggy from the blow he had taken to the head, he got up slowly onto his knees, and barely keeping his balance, he rose to his feet. He went over to the agent and turned him over with his foot. There was a gaping hole in his chest, blood seeping out, and Jake knew he was dead. He turned around and sat down with his back to the agent and with his hands behind him, fumbled in the agent's coat pockets. There were handcuff keys in his pocket. Jake got them out and after several attempts, was able to get the cuffs off. It seemed like it took forever. He dropped the keys at least twice during the effort, cursing as he did, but finally was able to free the cuffs from one of his wrists. Shaking his wrists to bring back the circulation, he brought the cuffs in front of him and took the other one off his wrist. He then reached over and picked up the agent's Beretta from where it had fallen. Slowly, he moved in the direction he heard the groans. Ortiz was alive, but had been shot in the gut, and he was half sitting against a carton, eyes closed. Jake kicked his feet. Ortiz's eyes opened, and he looked at Jake. Jake raised the Beretta, pointing it between Ortiz's eyes. For the first time, the smile left Ortiz's face and Jake actually believed he saw fear. Ortiz tried to speak but it was barely a mumble. Jake got closer. Ortiz's shirt was halfway open and his hand lay across his chest, moving back and forth on a cord like it was some kind of a rosary. "I have what you need in my trunk, man. It's in my trunk."

Jake reeled. The Butcher was trying to buy him off? With what, drug money? Jake stared long and hard. Jake made his decision. "Fuck it, this is for Annie," and calmly shot Ortiz between the eyes.

He went back to the dead agent, wiped the Beretta off with his shirttails, and put it in the agent's hand, clasping the hand around the butt. Jake moved to the window of the boathouse and looked outside. He didn't see any vehicles or any other agents in position, and when he was satisfied there was no one there, slowly opened the door and went out. He had been right. The only agent was the one who had been left to take care of Ortiz, and Jake made his way to the main house.

He walked in and looked over at Carrington, and even though he knew Carrington had helped the men who had tried to kill him, he felt some remorse for the passing of the person he had considered a friend. He searched and found Carrington's cell phone. It wasn't in the room where he heard Carrington talking. Going into that room, he saw that there was a conventional landline and knew that is what Carrington had used to make his calls. Jake opened the cell phone, retrieved its number, and wrote it down on a piece of paper. Pocketing the phone, he then went out front, closing the door behind him. There was wicker furniture on the front porch and Jake sat down in one of the chairs, rubbed his neck and his eyes, and leaned back and closed his eyes for a brief moment. Leaning forward, he opened the phone and punched in the numbers for the FBI switchboard in Miami.

The on-duty officer answered, "FBI."

"I need to route an emergency call to Mike Lang."

"Who's calling?"

"Look. I can't talk. It's an emergency. Get a hold of Lang and have him call this number. 305-629-8381."

"Sir, I can't . . ."

"Have him call the number." And Jake slammed the phone shut. All he could do now was sit and wait.

Fifteen minutes later, the phone rang. Jake flipped it open. "Hello."

"This is Agent Mike Lang. Who's this?"

"Listen, Lang, I've made complaints to you about this before. Now listen carefully."

"Who is this?"

"Just listen carefully. My granddad, lives at 428 Bay Road on Cudjoe Key, mile marker 20. Three houses up from him, there's been a lot of noise tonight. I've reported this I don't know how many times. I think the Cubans are coming. I think illegal immigrants from Cuba are coming ashore. I've tried to tell you this I don't know how many times and I'm getting real tired 'cause nobody wants to help me. But you know what, I'm worried about my old granddad. He can't even watch his games, you know—NFL? Now, are you going to help me or not?"

There was silence on the phone. Then Lang finally said, "The NFL, huh? I'll see what I can do." And Jake knew he understood.

CHAPTER 13

When he received the call from the FBI switchboard, Mike Lang was back in Key West, having taken a late night FBI flight from D.C. There were too many coincidences and Mike was starting to believe there was something to Jake's story. In one night, Jake's house had blown up, a girl he was involved with had been butchered, and now Jake's car had been found parked abandoned in the heart of Key West. That's why Mike returned the call to the anonymous caller that he had gotten from the switchboard. When the caller had first started talking, Mike was going to hang up and tell him he had more important things to do, but when he heard "NFL," then he knew the caller was Jake.

Instinct told Mike that it would be best if he went alone. He directed the agents to keep searching Duval Street and the other areas adjacent to it to see if any sign of Jake could be found, if anyone had seen him, and to talk to his friends and associates. Mike still wasn't sure what was going on or what he would find, but he put his car into gear and was on his way to Cudjoe Key.

Jake was half asleep when he heard the car coming up the road, pulling in two doors down from where he was sitting. He slowly got up. Staying out of the light and hugging the side of the buildings, he made his way down the yards until he could clearly see the car and could clearly see Mike Lang getting out of it. Mike was approaching the door of 428 when Jake whispered, "Mike, come over here." Lang's hand immediately went for his Glock.

"Mike, it's Jake."

Still keeping his hand on his weapon, Lang moved through the shadows until he came along side Jake. Looking at him and seeing his injuries, Lang said, "Jake, what the hell happened to you? Are you all right?"

"Yeah, I'm o.k. Come with me."

Silently, they walked the two doors down to Carrington's house and went inside.

"Here's fatality number one."

Mike went over and looked back at Jake. "Tom Carrington? You killed him?"

"No, no, no. I didn't kill him. He was killed by Matthews's men."

"What?! Jake, what happened here?"

"Sit down, Mike."

"Why'd you call me from a cell phone, and why the code words?"

"Mike, listen to what happened. You're gonna understand. For right now, I've got to be dead."

CHAPTER 14

Jake opened a couple of beers and they sat down. Jake went through the details of the whole night from meeting Annie and going home, the bomb, and the killer at his house.

"Wait a minute," Mike said, "I was at your house. There was no body found there."

"I'm sure there wasn't. I'm sure Matthews's men cleaned it up. But I'm telling you, I killed a guy. I stuck a piece of wood that was in this arm in his neck."

"All right, go ahead," Mike said.

Jake could hardly explain what had happened to Annie when he got to that point in the story, but made it through, and finished up with the gun battle he created between the agent and Ortiz.

"So, these two guys are down at the boathouse?"

"Yeah. Come on. We'll walk down."

Making their way to the boathouse, Jake, for the first time, paid attention to the car sitting outside. It was a souped up '68 GTO and from the rims and the paint job, he knew it had to be Ortiz's. It sure as hell wasn't the agent's and there were no other choices.

They moved into the boathouse and Jake showed Lang where the bodies were. After examining them, Mike said, "You're one lucky son of a bitch to get out of this one."

Jake shook his head. "Yeah, I'm real lucky. But we've got some work to do."

"What do you mean?"

"Look, as far as Matthews knows, I'm dead. I've got to stay dead so I can find a way, till hopefully *we* can find a way, to prove what happened."

"Jake, look, Matthews told you he's already got the story in place. The guy's going to be President of the United States. He has every powerful person in the world as his buddy. He's a hero. He's going to use everything at his disposal to manufacture evidence and all it's going to show is that Ortiz was his connection, his informant, he met him on a regular basis, and that Ortiz came after you and your girlfriend for what you had done to him. They're gonna say they got to you too late, and after you were dead, they killed Ortiz and one of the agents heroically died in the shootout. There's not going to be any evidence to support that Matthews is crazy and trying to take over the country, using drug money to do it."

Jake was walking in circles, rubbing the back of his neck, knowing that Lang's words were true, but determined that everything that had happened—him getting fired, losing his family, the deaths of Steve and Cindy Townsend, the death of Annie Lewis, the attempt to kill him . . . Matthews just wasn't going to get away with it.

"I know, I know," said Jake, "but there has to be something. There has to be a way. There has to be some evidence somewhere."

"I don't see it Jake. This guy's covered his tracks for a long time. He's good at it and he has the wherewithal to do it. At least one thing good has happened," said Lang, "this animal's done for. He won't be hurt'n anybody else."

Jake walked over to where Lang was standing, looking at Ortiz.

"No regrets about this guy, I take it?"

Jake looked at Lang. "No . . . none. He deserved to die. Mike, there's certain people that give up their rights to live in society. They ignore society's rules, they can't claim those rules in their favor when they want to. This guy was a butcher. He took delight in hurting people. Dead is the only place he should be."

Staring at Ortiz's body, Jake finally noticed. He remembered Ortiz fingering some cord around his neck like a rosary. "I have what you need in the trunk, man." Jake knelt down and moved the hand away and reached into Ortiz's shirt. It wasn't a cord. It was a rubber wire. Jake opened the shirt.

"It can't be."

"What?" Lang said.

Jake didn't answer. He rummaged through Ortiz's pockets and found the keys to his car. "C'mon." And he ran out the door.

Lang just shook his head and followed.

"Jake, what are you doing?"

"Come here. C'mon. C'mon."

Jake opened the trunk and rummaged inside, and there in the one corner was a briefcase. He went to open it, but it was locked.

"Shit."

"What is it, Jake?"

"I thought Ortiz was trying to buy me off."

"Maybe he was. It's probably full of drugs or money."

"No, I don't think so. Mike, he had on a wire. He was wired."

"What?"

Jake was fumbling with the key ring and finally he found the small key that didn't look like it fit anything in a car. He inserted it in the case and the tumblers clicked. Popping the clasp, he opened the lid and there it was. The case contained a custom piece of electronic equipment. Jake pressed eject, a cover popped open and a

CD was pushed forward. He reinserted the CD and pressed play.
And then he looked at Mike Lang and they both started to smile.

CHAPTER 15

It took another hour or so for them to take care of everything. They removed the wire from Ortiz's body and wiped the body down to try and get rid of any prints they might have made. They set the chair back up and put the cuff keys back in the agent's pocket. They closed and locked the trunk of Ortiz's car and put his car keys back in his pocket.

Jake took off his shirt and threw it into the bay, letting it float up against the shoreline. Back in the boathouse, Jake unbound his wound from the wood shard, and clenching his teeth, opened it up again. As it began to bleed, he held it over the chair and the floor around the chair and let the blood drops fall. He then re-bandaged the wound with a piece of his T-shirt.

When they were satisfied they had done everything they could, they went to Mike's car and left. They stopped at a bar on Sugar Loaf Key. Jake, wearing a baseball cap that Mike gave him pulled down low, went into a back booth in the bar. Looking around, they saw nothing out of the ordinary. Mike had taken off his suit jacket and tie and rolled up his shirtsleeves so as not to be too obvious. It was as safe a place as any, and they began to make their plans.

CHAPTER 16

It was almost daylight by the time Jake and Mike arrived at the Holiday Inn off of Roosevelt in Key West. Mike reserved a room in his name, indicating that he and one of his agents would be staying for the next two or three days. Once his FBI credentials were shown, there were no follow-up questions and he and Jake proceeded to the room.

"Look Jake, I have to go back out on the street, get my men together, coordinate with local law enforcement, call in the proper agencies, like the ATF, and do the follow-up investigation I would normally do in a case like this to make sure no one gets suspicious. With everything that's gone on, it's going to take some time, maybe the rest of the day. You look like shit. Why don't you try and get some rest and get your mind off things for a while? I'll try and get back here by early evening and we'll go from there."

Jake replied, "I feel like shit. In fact, I feel like I've been through a war. I think I'll take you up on that. Are you sure you don't need me for anything?"

"No, Jake. Look, you were right. You've got to stay out of this from here on in. Remember, everyone thinks you're dead, and that's the way we have to play this. I'll take care of everything and, hopefully, when I comeback I can call in my final report and get it sent up to Washington."

"Alright, then I'll see you later," said Jake.

After Lang left, Jake sank onto the bed, more tired than he had ever felt in his life. He lay back and within seconds, he was sound asleep.

Jake sat bolt upright, wide-awake, when he heard the noise. He had to focus for a second before he realized it was only Mike entering the room.

"Well, hello Sleeping Beauty."

"Very funny," said Jake, looking at the clock. It was 4:00 p.m. He had slept almost ten hours. "How'd it go?"

"We did all the due diligence we would do in any investigation. I had some of my guys go up to Cudjoe to do an analysis of the crime scene, make sure all of the blood was picked up and labeled. We discussed what probably happened, with me giving them my point of view, and that's pretty much what everybody agreed with. The ATF will be looking at the bombing of your apartment, and I've made contact with the local authorities about Annie. No one knows about the Townsends yet so I didn't bring that up—thought it would be better to do later, after we see how this all plays out."

The thought of Steve Townsend and his wife struck Jake hard again and he sat slumped on the bed. Finally, he said, "Well, where do we go from here?"

"I want you to listen while I call this in," as Mike dialed his cell phone. "This is Mike Lang filing a report on activities in Key West this past weekend. On notification from the Attorney General's Office, it was determined that one Jake Sullivan, a person of interest in a separate potential indictment, was under threat of bodily harm in the vicinity of Key West and the lower Keys. I and two other agents responded and found the following: 1) The suspect's home had been damaged in what appeared to be a bomb blast early Sunday morning. The subject was not found at the scene, nor were other parties or suspects identified; 2) The subject's vehicle was found abandoned on Green Street in Key West, but the subject was not located during a search of Duval Street and surrounding areas; 3) An anonymous report was received about noises in the vicinity of number 428 at the Cudjoe Key Marina on Cudjoe Bay. On investigation, it appeared that there was no activity at the given address, but two doors down an unidentified vehicle was spotted. Further investigation led to the following: A) The owner of the residence, Thomas Carrington, former Sheriff of Monroe County was found dead, within his home, due to a gunshot wound. B) In the boathouse on the aforesaid property, two bodies were found: one Agent Samuel Miller, and one Carlos Ortiz, a former suspect in the South Beach Sadist slayings, who had been prosecuted by Jake Sullivan when he was Chief Prosecutor in the U.S. Attorney's Office in Miami. Both the agent and Ortiz were dead of gunshot wounds; C) A chair was also found in the boathouse with signs that a person had been seated in the chair with his arms handcuffed behind him. There was blood on the chair and around the chair and on a razor, which was found near the body of Ortiz. Given the M.O. of the crimes of which Ortiz was suspected, the following reconstruction was made: Because of his prosecution by Sullivan, Ortiz tracked him to Key West, where he attempted to eliminate him, first by attempting to run him down while Sullivan was on a bicycle, said incident having been reported by Sullivan previously to this agent, then by attempting to eliminate Sullivan in a bombing at his residence/office, and finally it is believed that Sullivan was murdered by Ortiz in the boathouse on the Carrington property and then dumped in Cudjoe Bay. The blood found at the scene will be tested to match Sullivan's DNA. Additionally, a shirt was found in Cudjoe Bay with blood on it, which will also be tested and compared to Sullivan's DNA. It is presumed that the agent in question was also following the lead received by the duty officer at FBI Headquarters in Miami and came upon Ortiz after his murder of Sullivan and shots were exchanged, killing both the agent and Ortiz. Dredging operations of Cudjoe Bay will commence to try and recover Sullivan's body and, until DNA tests and dredging operations are concluded, he will be considered missing and not officially dead, although it appears that a murder has been committed. There has been no further sighting of Sullivan since these events."

Jake listened while his demise was recorded and when Lang hung up, said, "Very nice job of reporting me dead."

"Fits in with the plan, you have to admit. And now we have to hope everything else works, also."

"You sure you have agents that you can trust?"

"Yeah. I have a core group of guys that I think I can depend on pretty well once I lay out the scenario."

"Look, before you leave, let me get a shower and change into the clothes we bought at that all-night joint. Then we'll go get some dinner and go to the copy center."

"You sure you want to do it this way?"

"Look, if I tell anyone I'm alive, including Eva, I could put them in danger. I don't know what phones are tapped and I don't know where people are looking for me, but I wouldn't put anything past Matthews. I have to stay dead, and for everyone to think I'm dead, I have to act like I am."

"Yeah, you're right. It's the only way to go right now."

Jake felt immensely better after a quick shower. He re-wrapped his left arm, put on the T-shirt and shorts he had bought at one of the all-night T-shirt shops that lined the Keys. He used the electric razor he purchased to give himself a crew cut. He appeared quite different without the usual shaggy mane he sported living in Key West. His stubble of beard, flip-flops, and a pair of sunglasses completed the outfit. He thought that unless he ran into someone who actually knew him very well, he would look like an average Keys tourist, or just another resident living the good life.

Jake and Lang had dinner at the diner next door, and when they were done, using Lang's credit card, they went to the copy store and made three copies of the disc they found in Ortiz's brief-case. Jake had taken the briefcase, put the original CD back in the player, and locked it. They visited several other stores including a men's clothing store, where Jake bought a complete suit of clothes, including shirt, tie, a two-piece lightweight suit, belt, socks, and shoes—all with Lang's credit card.

Finally, they stopped at Enterprise Rent-A-Car, where Lang rented a car in his name. Before leaving the Enterprise lot, they sat in Lang's car, and Jake asked, "How much time do you think we have?"

"The dredging operation is going to take some time—prob-ably a couple of days, and there may be a body in there that we do find from some other source, but it sure as hell isn't going to be yours. Identification, *if* it is possible, is also gonna take some time, so I'd say that's not going to be a problem. A DNA test will certainly show it's your blood, so all in all, I think Matthews is going to think his plan worked and you're no longer with us."

"Mike, are you sure you can get to see him?"

"I think so. I told you I have an in and the guy owes me, so, hopefully, it will work out."

"What if it doesn't?"

"If it doesn't, we have a problem. Matthews has too much clout. I can't do anything through the Bureau or through the Department that he's not going to know about. This is the only way this is going to work. If Matthews gets wind of this, there are going to be agents swarming all over you and me. Then they're gonna find what we have and when they do, this is over. What you have to do is stay out of sight as much as you can. You're just going to have to wait it out until I can get in touch with you. Remember, only call my personal cell phone. As far as I know, that number is not used in any official capacity and it isn't monitored. Since the new guy's been in office he did away with the Patriot Act and the eavesdropping that Bush had in place, so I think it's safe. Use that throw away—they are very hard to trace. And you know what to say to get my attention. All we can do is hope the schedule permits a meeting and he's still in town. All right?"

"Yep, you got it. I'll take care of what you wanted done on my end and I'll have it ready."

"Good. You call me when it's done and I'll tell you where to send it. Start on it as soon as you can so I have it when I need it."

"I know."

"All right. Get out of the car and get to work. I'm heading back to Miami."

"All right, Mike." With that, Jake got out of the car and walked toward the rental. Halfway there he turned back and walked back to Mike's driver's side window just as he was pulling out of the parking lot.

"What'd you forget?"

"Nothing Mike. I just wanted to say thanks for being there for me again."

"Just get done what I said to get done."

"Yes, sir."

And with that, Mike was gone. Jake got in the rental car and drove back to the Holiday Inn, unloaded the items they had purchased, and went to his room. Sitting on the bed, he stared at the mini bar and realized how much he wanted a beer. He sat there for a long time, just staring. He finally got up and dialed room service, "Would you mind sending over a six-pack of Diet Coke and bucket of ice?" While waiting, Jake hung up his newly purchased clothing, set out the legal pads and pens he had purchased, the throwaway mobile phone, and put the new toiletries in the bathroom. Finally, he unlocked and rechecked Ortiz's briefcase. There was a knock at the door and Jake moved to get the gun Mike had given him. It was under the blanket covering the pillows on the bed, but he checked himself.

"Who is it?" he asked.

"Room Service, Sir. Your Diet Cokes are here."

He opened the door and there was a young man pushing a cart with a glass and several Diet Cokes on a tray.

"C'mon in."

The young man rolled the tray into the room. As Jake turned to get money from his wallet, the young man reached under the apron over the cart. The movement caught Jake's attention and he dove for the bed, put his hand under the pillow, and yanked out the revolver, only to see the young man with a horrified look on his face, drop the bucket of ice all over the top of the tray. Jake immediately put the gun down.

"I'm sorry, kid, I'm sorry. I'm with the FBI. We are on a case and everything's a little tense. You have to excuse me." Jake had hoped the young man hadn't wet himself, gave him an extra tip, and apologized again, as the young man backed out of the room and closed the door. "Way to go, Jake," he thought.

Gathering up the ice, he put it back in the bucket, and poured himself a cold glass of Diet Coke. There was one more thing he had to do before he sat down at the desk. As agreed upon, he took the small screwdriver he had purchased, took the desk chair, moved it over to the wall, and climbed up. He unscrewed the cover of the air conditioning vent, then he took one of the discs placed it into a jewel box and set it inside the vent. He re-screwed the cover into place and checked to make sure there were no obvious marks on the screws, and then checked the floor below to make sure that there were no traces of plaster dust or anything else to indicate that the cover had been removed. Jake sure hoped the CD would still be there after all was said and done. The only reason for hiding it was so that Mike could find it if Matthews got to Jake first. He took the chair back to the desk, and taking a long drink of Diet Coke, he collected his thoughts and began. When he was finished, he looked at the clock. It was almost 3:00 a.m.. on Monday morning, but he had written out a complete statement of what had occurred, beginning with his drive home from Miami until the present—leaving out scaring the busboy half to death. There wasn't anything else to do, so he lay back down on the bed and stared at the ceiling.

MONDAY

CHAPTER 17

It was the throwaway cell phone ringing that woke him up. He looked at the clock and again realized how tired he must have been, for it was now 8:00 a.m. He grabbed the phone from the nightstand."

"Yeah?"

"Is it done?"

"Yeah. I have it here."

"All right. Here's the number I want you to fax it to."

"Just a second," Jake said as he got a pad and pencil. "Go."

"305-472-8369. Do it within the next five minutes. I'm standing beside the machine."

"All right, I will. Call when you get it."

Jake shut the phone, put on his flip-flops, and headed down to the lobby. Looking around to make sure there was nothing out of the ordinary, or more importantly—no one out of the ordinary, Jake asked if he could use the fax machine and was directed to "the business center," where a fax/copier and a computer were available for the benefit of guests. The cost was 25¢ per page and Jake had to go back to the counter to get the necessary change to send it through. Dropping in ten quarters, he put the pages in the tray, entered the fax number, and sent it on its way.

He looked at the young lady at the desk and asked, "Does this fax send a confirmation that it was received?"

"Yes, sir. It usually comes a few seconds after you send the fax."

"Thank you."

Jake waited anxiously. Finally, the beeping, confirming transmission, sounded and he reached down and saw that the fax had gone to the number indicated. As he was walking back to the room, the cell phone rang.

"Did you get it?"

"Yeah, its here."

"Did you call yet?"

"No, I waited until I got this. I'm gonna call now."

"Let me know."

"I will."

Back in his room, Jake couldn't go back to sleep. Although he had to admit the rest had done him some good, he decided to take another long shower, properly shave, and make himself as presentable as he could. While shaving, Jake accidentally nicked himself. Damn, he thought, as he touched his face and pulled his hand away with blood. He looked at himself in the mirror. There *is* blood on my hands. He thought about Annie and the Townsends, even about Carrington. He was responsible for their deaths—all of them. He knew Annie had died horribly and was sure the Townsends had met a similar fate. He had seen Carrington die, but his thoughts kept coming back to Annie. There was no getting around it. He knew he wasn't the bad guy, but he still knew he was responsible. His reflections were interrupted by the ringing of the cell phone. Toweling off the shaving cream, he went to the nightstand and picked up.

"Hello?"

There was silence on the other end. Alarm started to seep into Jake's gut and a voice finally came from the other end.

"It's me. Jake, I got a call from Eva."

This is what Jake had been dreading. He sat down on the edge of the bed.

"How'd it go?"

"The rumors about you are all over Key West. You're either dead or missing, or both. Naturally, she was hysterical. I tried to calm her down and explain to her that we have no evidence that you're dead and we aren't sure whether you just decided to get away for a while or if something happened. Naturally, she reminded me of what had happened to you on the bicycle and the fact that your house and office were blown up, which made it difficult for me to calm her down. I explained to her that I was personally working the case and that she could call me at any time and *should* call me, should anyone ask about you. She did give me one reason to think we're playing this right. She told me that she noticed a car sitting out in front of her house most of the morning and that when she went outside on her porch and looked at the driver, he simply drove away."

Jake said, "As we figured, Matthews is probably covering his bases to see if I show up anywhere."

"That's my thought, too," said Lang.

"What about the other thing?"

"I made my initial inquiry and I added an addendum to your statement and passed it on. I'm waiting to hear back. Hopefully, we'll get the o.k., and if we do, you should be ready to move fast."

"I'm in the middle of taking a shower now. I thought when I was done I'd just get in the car and drive to Miami."

Lang thought for a while. "That's not a bad idea, as long as you have the cell phone and I can direct you wherever I need you to go, no matter what happens. You should be o.k. on the road, given the rental car and the way you look."

"All right. I'll get finished and take off. I'm not going to check out, though. I'll just leave things as is. We'll worry about that later."

"Good idea. Keep me posted."

"I will. Wish me luck."

"You have it."

And with that, they hung up. Jake finished shaving and brushing his teeth, and climbed into a hot shower, where he stayed much longer than usual. It helped with some of the aches and pains and cleared the cobwebs out of his head. When he was done, he toweled off for a long while and then began to dress. Luckily, Jake was a straight size 44 regular and no alterations were needed to the suit coat or pants that he bought. Looking in the mirror he thought that for a cheap purchase he didn't look too shabby. Hopefully, he would be presentable enough if things worked out as he and Mike had planned. Gathering up the cell phone, the legal pad and pens and the extra discs, he put them in the case that held the recording device. He was ready to leave when he went back to the bed, reached under the pillow, pulled out the weapon, and stuck it in his belt at the small of his back. He then went to the door and opened it enough for him to see down the hall. Empty. He stuck his head out enough to see in the other direction and found the same. Quickly, he exited, shut the door, and made for the elevator. He rode down alone, went out one of the side entrances, and then around to the parking lot where he had parked the rental car. He got in and sat down, senses alert for anything that seemed out of place—any sound, any movement. There was nothing. He waited approximately 15 minutes—out of an abundance of caution— then started the car and retraced his route around the parking lot to see if anyone had hidden behind him. Seeing no one, he pulled out into traffic, but instead of heading north to go up the Keys, he went south on Roosevelt, making a left just before Old Town. He stopped at a convenience store and bought a Diet Coke and came back out to the car. Again, nothing seemed out of place. He saw no new car that had not been there when he went in. Backing out of the parking lot, he went back the way he had come. No one pulled over; no car made any unusual movements; and no car looked like a government issue.

Feeling he was as safe as he could be, he made the left at Roosevelt onto U.S. 1 and headed north. It was a beautiful day. The sun was bright, the air was a little bit cool, but not so much that he didn't crack the windows to let it come in. He could smell the salt and the sea air that came in from both sides of the Keys. He tensed as he drove past Cudjoe Key and again at Bahia Honda. He only passed one Highway Patrol car going in the opposite direction, and half expected it to turn around and start chasing him, but it didn't happen. Pulling into Holiday Isle on Islamorada to use the facilities, he went to the Tiki Bar, the previous yearning of the day not having gone away. Again, however, he ordered a Diet Coke to go and got back in the car.

He had just hit Florida City at the end of the Keys when the cell phone rang.

"Yeah?"

"We're good to go."

Jake let out an audible sigh of relief. "What do I do?"

"All right, listen. I want you to go to Miami International. Go toward the parking area at Terminal B. You'll see a sign that says "Restricted Take Off." Follow that sign. You will be on a road with different gate numbers. Go to Gate 2 and I'll meet you at the gate."

"You mean he's actually going to see us?"

"That's the plan."

"Mike, how the hell did you pull this off?"

"I told you. There are some people that owed me some favors and I called them in."

"They must have been some pretty goddamn big favors."

"I'll explain it to you later. Just get to the airport."

"I'm on my way."

Jake looked at his watch. It was 11:15. He should be at Miami International by noon. Jake was on Interstate 75 when he saw the sign for Miami International and pulled off the exit ramp.

Following Mike's directions, he followed the signs for Terminal B and almost missed the sign for restricted takeoffs, and narrowly avoided cutting off another car, swinging into the proper lane. He waved an "I'm sorry" to the other driver, who Jake knew wouldn't be too happy with his actions. He ended up on a small road with a fence on the left-hand side. Finally, he saw Gate 1, passed it, and came to Gate 2. As he pulled up, Lang appeared and swung open the two gates so the car could enter. Jake pulled in and parked next to where Lang had parked his vehicle and got out. He opened the trunk and took out the briefcase.

"Well, my man, are you ready?"

"Ready as I'm ever gonna be."

"All right, let's do this."

They walked to where the jet was idling on the tarmac.

"How'd you rate this?"

"The FBI has these jets at their disposal and I filed a flight plan that I had to go into the Justice Department 'cause I personally wanted to transfer DNA samples from the crime scene to the lab. Matthews knows our history. He would expect me to stay on top of this, especially if he thinks that I think that you're dead."

"Sounds like you thought it out pretty well."

"Look, we're playing this as we go. The big thing is we have to keep Matthews thinking everything is working out fine. Otherwise, he'll start his countermove, and that's what we don't want to have happen. Once he covers his tracks, they'll be buried forever and we're done."

"I know. I just hope what we have is convincing enough."

CHAPTER 18

Lang walked back from the cockpit. "We should be in D.C. around 2:00 o'clock," he said and sat down opposite Jake. They flew in silence for a while when Lang turned to Jake. "I'm sorry about your woman friend that got killed. Were you two close?"

Jake sighed heavily. "I'd seen her around Key West off and on for a number of years, but only asked her out a couple weeks ago."

"Was it serious?"

"Not really. We hadn't had time to make it serious. I think maybe she wanted it that way, but you know, the truth is, Mike, I'm still in love with Linda. Somewhere I keep thinking that this is all going to work out and things are going to go back to the way they were."

"Well, she never got a divorce so, maybe she's thinking the same thing."

"I don't know. There's a lot of hurt there. I let our family collapse."

"Yeah, but now you found out it wasn't your fault."

"Losing the evidence and losing the job wasn't my fault, but the way I reacted to it, the way I treated Linda and the girls, that was my fault."

"Don't beat yourself up too bad," said Mike. "Something like that happens, everything you've worked for goes south, it's hard to take."

"It's not just that. Linda was there for me. She tried. She kept working to make ends meet. She took care of the kids. She tried to make them understand what I was going through. She did it all . . . and I didn't do anything. I sat there stewing in my own self-pity and ruined it all."

"I don't know Jake. The way this has played out, maybe this is your second chance."

Jake stared out the window watching the white clouds underneath the blue canopy, stretched out like a bag of cotton balls spilled on blue cloth. Finally, he said, "The truth of it is I don't even know if I deserve a second chance." Again, there was silence.

"Mike," said Jake, "why didn't you ever marry?"

Mike laughed. "I'm married to the job. Too many odd hours, too many odd events. It's hard to get close to someone, and on a moment's notice, no matter what the situation you're in, you have to walk out the door and they have to worry about you ever coming back."

"Do you ever wish you'd made some other choice? Done something else?"

"Oh hell, I don't know. Always wanted to play shortstop for the Yankees and then Jeter ruined that."

They both laughed.

"You know, Jake, I don't know how much of this we plan. I graduated from college, went to law school, and realized that I wasn't like you. I didn't really like the law. I didn't like all the paperwork. I didn't like all the deals. That's when I applied to the Bureau, and here I am. When I first started, was that something I wanted to do? Na, I didn't think about it. But it's the way it worked out."

Jake thought for a long time. He remembered when he was at Allegheny. It was back in the 60's—days of peace and love, and he thought about becoming a history professor at some college in New England, buying a stone farmhouse and living off the land in rural, New Hampshire. Then the summer after he graduated, he met Linda, who was going to a state teachers college in southwestern Pennsylvania. They met in August and Jake was drafted and entered the service in September. Those two events within the space of a month changed everything. He fell in love with Linda right away and he knew she was the person he wanted to marry. He asked her on his first leave home from the Army and she said yes. He did his basic at Fort Dix and then went to Fort Monmouth, where he got stuck in the legal department. Vietnam was winding down. Peace talks were going on and Jake was one of the members of the last draft. He kept having orders cut to Fort Ord, to fly overseas, but nothing ever came of it. He stayed at Fort Monmouth the rest of his time, and not knowing what to do at that point in his life, decided to go to law school on the GI Bill. He went to Duquesne University in Pittsburgh at night and found himself able to cut through all the normal garbage that young law students go through to get to the point of things. Maybe it was because he was older, maybe it was because of the Army—he didn't know. But it came pretty easily to him. He was first in his class the first two years and finished third. The last year was tough. That was the year his mom died of cancer. Jake was holding down a day job and going to law school at night. Linda and he got married right before he got out of the Army. She had graduated that summer and was getting some teaching jobs, but she was also working odd jobs at bakeries, cleaners, and clothing stores so they could make ends meet. They were so much in love, and even though they didn't have anything, life seemed rich, so enjoyable. They laughed and kidded about being two ships in the night because of their strange hours coming and going between school and work. When Jake graduated, he got a job in the U.S. Attorney's Office in Pittsburgh and again things just worked out. The Chief Assistant was prosecuting a case with a high political profile involving the Allegheny County Sheriff's Office when he became severely ill and Jake had to step in and take over. He won that case and went on to a string of successes, winning every case he tried. At the same time, the girls were born five years apart, Jennifer first and then Jessica, and he had everything in life he wanted, especially when the opening came up in Miami and he and Linda and the girls decided to take it.

He felt a slight nudge on his shoulder. "Jake, Jake." It was Mike.

"Yeah, what is it?"

"You all right?"

"Yeah, just thinking about things."

"Well, we'll be there shortly. Get your thoughts collected as to what you're going to say. We've got to close this deal." And Jake's thoughts came back to the moment at hand. They landed at approximately 2:00 o'clock in Washington, D.C., where another black vehicle with tinted glass awaited them. They were ushered in and off they went. It was still relatively warm in D.C., Jake thought as they passed by monuments and marble buildings.

"It's been a while since I've been here," he said to Mike.

"I've found that this is a good place to stay away from. This place is filled with bureaucrats are who don't know one thing about how things outside this city work."

Jake laughed and looked at Mike. "And this is where we're coming for help?"

Mike shot him a glance, amused at the situation they found themselves in. They came to the gate. The driver identified them and they were ushered in.

"Amazing, all the times I've seen this place from afar, on television or in photos, but I've never noticed the detail."

It was truly imposing. They came to the top of the drive, the car stopped and they were ushered out. Their credentials were checked once again, and they were escorted through a door and down a hallway. After making several turns, they came to a doorway and their escort asked them to wait while he went inside. A moment later, he ushered them in, and there they stood, in the center of power of the United States and perhaps the whole world. Directly in front of them rising from his desk, was Jordan Fletcher, the President of the United States.

"Agent Lang, good to meet you."

"Mr. President."

"And you, I take it, are Jake Sullivan."

"It's an honor, Mr. President."

"Come over by the desk and have a seat, gentlemen."

Jake was almost rooted to the spot. He couldn't believe he was in the Oval Office in the White House, talking to the President of the United States, but here he was, and he knew he had to get back that old prosecutorial fire to make his case to the one man who could help bring down Benjamin Matthews.

"Mr. Sullivan, I've read your signed statement, and I must tell you that under other circumstances I would never believe a word of it, and you would never be sitting where you are right now. Agent Lang, I know that you are a close friend of Aaron Young, the head of my secret service detail, and I must tell you that I hold him in great regard, which is one reason you're here. Don't get me wrong, I think Benjamin Matthews was a mistake . . . my mistake. I think he has become emboldened by the power of his office and has a desire for even more power. I know he intends to run against me next year and I know that given his public reputation, he has a good chance of winning. I deeply fear, however, what could happen to this country should that event occur, even without the information you've put before me. But what you have given me, even if I were to believe you, is not sufficient evidence for me to initiate an action against the Attorney General of the United States. So, gentlemen, you have a sympathetic ear. Convince me."

Mike spoke up first. "Mr. President, I'd like Mr. Sullivan to present our case to you. He went through everything first hand, as you know from his statement, and he has additional information to present to you."

"Very well. Mr. Sullivan, you may begin."

And Jake did. He went through everything, starting with his drive back to Key West, and when he was finished, the President said, "So, Mr. Sullivan, you're telling me that you have Benjamin Matthews on tape detailing his involvement with the drug cartels in Colombia and Mexico and his plans for the future of this country?"

"If I may, Mr. President." Jake got the briefcase from where he had set it beside his chair and set it on top of the Resolute Desk, the desk that had been used by Presidents since the time Queen Victoria had presented it as a gift to President Hayes in 1880.

Jake, didn't need to check, he was prepared. He pressed play. When it was over, the President stood and walked to the window overlooking the Rose Garden, he turned and said, "Gentlemen, particularly you, Mr. Sullivan, on behalf of the United States, I want to apologize for the ordeal you have been through, and thank you for bringing this information to me. I believe your actions have saved the United States from grievous injury. I have no doubt that Benjamin Matthews fully intended to carry out this plot and without your actions, may well have been successful, which would have resulted in the destruction of our freedoms and God knows what else. Now, if you have no objection, I'd like to call in my Chief of Staff so that we can determine how we should proceed."

With that, President Fletcher pushed the intercom. "Diana, have Jason Bates come into my office right away."

A moment later, a side panel of the Oval Office opened and in walked Jason Bates, Chief of Staff for President Fletcher. After the introductions were made, the President outlined what he had heard and explained the proof.

"Jason, the concern is that Matthews, if he gets wind of what's going on, will cover his tracks. Once this stuff is made public, the odds are it will ruin his chances to become President, but doesn't necessarily mean a prosecution would be successful, or that the drug trafficking business would stop. I want this man put away. I consider his action treasonous and I don't want him to get away with it."

Bates spoke. "Mr. President, we can clearly go to the Federal Court and get a warrant for his arrest. I can handle that myself. And I think we can be assured that no judge is going to get involved politically with Matthews at this point, not with this about to come crashing down on him. Once we have those documents, we need to move in and make the arrest, but that's where I'm a little concerned. The U.S. Marshals report directly to the Attorney General."

The President spoke up. "Agent Lang, do you have a group of agents you can depend on, that you know are not compromised in any way?"

"I do, sir. I can round up a team to serve the warrants and make the arrests."

"Then that's the way we should go," said Bates. "We keep the information limited to as few people as possible and we proceed with due speed."

"Let me check one thing," said the President. And again, he went to the intercom. "Diana, do me a favor. Check the guest list for that gala at the Kennedy Center I have to go to tonight and see if the Secretary of Health, Education and Welfare, the Secretary of Commerce, and the Attorney General are on that list and get back to me."

The President looked at the puzzled faces before him. "I don't give a damn if the other two are coming or not, but I don't want to pinpoint the Attorney General."

It only took a moment for the intercom to buzz.

"What? All right, thank you Diana. Matthews is scheduled to be there, which means he's in Washington." And the President looked at Bates. "Jason, I want this done by 5:00 o'clock this afternoon. That gives you roughly two hours. Nothing to the press until after it's completed, and then we'll make a very non-specific statement until we can do a full investigation. I want your team to do that too, Agent Lang. Can you do it?"

Both Bates and Lang replied "Yes, Mr. President."

"Mr. Sullivan, I want to once again thank you for your service. If you will you give that briefcase and other information to Mr. Bates, we will proceed."

It was now or never, thought Jake. "Mr. President, if I may, I have a small favor to ask of you."

The President sat back at his desk. "And what might that be?"

Fifteen minutes later, the President sat looking back from Jake to Mike. "Agent Lang, do you vouch for this man?"

"I do, sir."

"Mr. Sullivan, you know the significance of what you are asking me to do?"

"I do, Mr. President."

"Jason, what do you think?"

During Jake's presentation, Bates had been looking hard at him, and now he looked to the President. "Given the circumstances, Mr. President, I think it's a request that should be honored."

The President again looked at Jake and slowly began to nod his head. "I think I agree, Jason. Very well, Mr. Sullivan. I'm entrusting you with this part of this project and we will work out the details of the remainder of your request if everything goes as we hope it does. Is that fair?"

"Absolutely, Mr. President, and thank you."

"All right gentlemen, let's move on this, and for my part, I'm going to get the Presidents of Colombia and Mexico on the phone and tell them they have a problem in their governments they need to take care of."

With that, the meeting was over, Jason Bates went out the way he had come in, and Jake and Mike exited the door they had come in, immediately being picked up by their escort, who had been waiting outside. They said nothing until they had exited the White House, went back to their vehicle, heading to FBI headquarters.

"So when did you decide?" said Mike.

"I think just sitting there in the Oval Office. It's like you said. Things just work out a certain way. Sometimes you've got to give them a little push."

Mike shook his head and started laughing, "That was a hell of a push."

CHAPTER 19

A messenger from Bates' office arrived at approximately 4:00 p.m. with the warrants. Mike opened the envelope and looked at them.

"Did he get it?"

Mike finished reading and looked up. "It's here."

"Let's go. Make the call."

Mike picked up the phone. "All right, it's a go." He hung up the phone and motioned to Jake. "C'mon. Let's go."

By 4:30, there were three vehicles sitting on a side street, and the occupants were watching the entrance of the Justice Department across the street at 950 Pennsylvania Avenue. In the lead vehicle were two agents with Mike and Jake in the back. Finally, Jake couldn't stand the waiting any longer. "Do you think it worked? Do you see him?"

"It will work, Jake, and no, I don't see him yet."

Several more minutes passed.

"There he is."

A man had come out of the front entrance of the Justice Department dressed in a sport coat, shirt, and tie, and made his way down Pennsylvania Avenue, went past them, crossed the street, and then made his way back into the side street where they were parked. He came around to Mike's window.

"Well?"

"It's all taken care of. We took the mail clerk into custody, and I took his cart and made my way around the offices. I had plenty of letters directed to Matthews. I waited out in the corridor pretending to be sorting mail until Matthews left the office. Then, I went in and put a pile of letters on his desk, making sure that the presidential seal on the letter from the President was just visible sticking out from under the top envelope. Then I took care of the other little details we had discussed, so you should have no problem from here on out.

"Good work."

"Thank you, sir."

"All right everybody, let's go."

And with that, Mike, Jake, and ten agents got out of their vehicles and dispersed onto Pennsylvania Avenue, approaching the Justice Department from different directions so it didn't appear like an invading army. One group of agents went to the communications center to make sure no warnings were sounded. A second group covered underground escape routes to transportation, and another group made sure that all surface exits were covered. Mike and Jake and two other agents headed up the elevator to the office of the Attorney General.

Matthews was sitting in his office, smiling at the invitation he received from the President of the United States to attend a state dinner next week. Typical, thought Matthews, country's going to hell and all this clown wants to do is have dinners. Things were certainly about to change. And that's when his door opened.

"Agent Lang, it's nice to see you, but why didn't Alicia ring you in?"

"Alicia's no longer present, sir."

"What are you talking about?" said Matthews, and pressed the intercom button. "Alicia . . . Alicia."

"Sir, she's not there."

"What the hell is going on, and how dare you burst into my office like this!"

"Benjamin Matthews, I have a letter from the President of the United States requesting your immediate resignation and a warrant for your arrest, as well as a search warrant for your office, and all other offices of the Justice Department."

"What the hell are you talking about?"

Mike handed him the documents and Matthews looked them over in cursory fashion and threw them on his desk. "This is all about that crap down in Florida? About me meeting with Ortiz? I explained that to you. He was a confidential informant and I know, I know, he did some horrible things, none of which, by the way, I was aware of, including this last episode involving that woman and Jake Sullivan. I know you were friends with Sullivan and I'm sorry."

"You ought to read the warrant carefully, sir. You're being charged with murder, attempted murder, drug trafficking, and treason in the form of crimes and misdemeanors against the United States of America."

"You're out of your goddamn mind! You think you can come in here with this shit and threaten me? I'm the Attorney General of the United States and I'm going to be the next President of the United States. You have no evidence for any of this. Fletcher is trying to save his ass. He knows I'm going to beat him next year. This is a political vendetta, with you because your friend died, and him because he's going to lose this country. Now get out of my office before I get a team of U.S. Marshals up here to arrest your ass!"

"Sir, you're mistaken. We do have evidence."

"What? That CD that Jake Sullivan made? And tell me, what's it show? Me with a bunch of my agents meeting with Ortiz in the Florida Keys? Yeah, that's exactly what it shows. Ortiz was giving me further information to allow me to win this war on drugs and we met there because that's where he wanted to meet. It was for his protection, and if you check out the logbooks and check out my agents, you'll see it's something that was done by me or my assistant on numerous occasions. Same meeting place . . . same reason . . . with detailed log-ins of the information that was provided and the arrests and convictions it led to. You're gonna try and tell me that constitutes some type of crime?"

"No sir, that's not the evidence I'm talking about."

"Then what the fuck evidence are you talking about?"

"This evidence." And with that, Jake Sullivan walked into the room.

CHAPTER 20

It was only momentary, but there was a look of disbelief and fear in Matthews's eyes, and then he was right back with the same bravado. "Jake, thank God you're alive! We all thought you were dead."

"You mean you thought you had killed me," said Jake.

"Sorry, Agent Lang. The existence of Mr. Sullivan here doesn't constitute evidence—just that he's one lucky son of a bitch." Matthews started chuckling and went back and sat behind his desk. "All right boys, I'll play the game. How'd you do it, Jake? How'd you get away?"

Jake recounted the events at the boathouse and Matthews shook his head accordingly. "Not bad for a former federal prosecutor. The shirt in the bay was a nice touch. So was the blood—DNA showed it was yours. Figured this was a done deal. But why the charade?"

"To keep you from backtracking, you son of a bitch . . . make sure you didn't destroy evidence like you've done through this whole thing to get yourself off the hook."

"Gentlemen, I don't know what you're talking about, but you can check any records you want to. This is an open administration, as the President has indicated, and I'm happy to comply with any requests for information or any of my records. You see boys, I have nothing to hide. And Jake, I'm sorry you think I was somehow involved in this attempt to take your life, and I do apologize for the actions of Mr. Ortiz. We thought we could control him and we obviously couldn't. And I'm sorry for the loss of that sweet young woman in Key West."

"Yeah, and are you sorry for the loss of Tom Carrington? And are you sorry for the loss of Steve and Cindy Townsend, too?"

"As I understand it, Mr. Carrington died as a result of you leading Ortiz to his house. And it's just as well. He was under investigation for accepting bribes, so he was about to take a fall anyway. This will spare his friends and his family that type of distasteful business. And I think you'll find the coroner's report and other evidence clearly indicate that Steve Townsend killed his wife and then took his own life 'cause he could no longer conduct the fraudulent enterprise you and he were engaged in. And as a matter of fact, Jake, you're still under investigation yourself for those issues, and I'm afraid we're going to have to prosecute."

Jake had had enough. He rushed the desk, slammed both palms down, and got within inches of Matthews's face. "You arrogant son of a bitch! You caused the death of more people than I can count and you sit here and talk about prosecutions! The only prosecution that's gonna happen is yours! And I guarantee you . . . I guarantee you . . . you're going down for everything you've done!"

Matthews sat there calmly and then leaned forward. "Jake, you always have the same problem. No evidence." And with that, he stood up. "Now, if you boys will excuse me, I have work to do," and he threw the warrants in the trash basket.

"Matthews," Jake said, "you remember that day that we were going to prosecute Ortiz?"

"You mean the day you fucked up the case, Jake, by losing the evidence that would have allowed us to prosecute Ortiz?"

"You remember the briefcase and evidence in the trunk of my car?"

"I don't remember reading about it in the reports, but I remember having fired you because of gross negligence."

"The briefcase full of evidence, Matthews. It was going to bring down a monster." He looked at Mike. "Life's funny, isn't it?"

"Fuck'n hilarious," said Lang.

"Here's another briefcase, Matthews. Another briefcase full of evidence that's going to bring down a monster."

Again, Jake could see it. There was a wary look in Matthews's eyes. "Now what are you talking about?"

"Just listen." And with that, Jake opened the briefcase and pressed play. Benjamin Matthews heard his own voice detailing the crimes he had committed and his plans for the country. When it was done, Jake pressed stop and held up the CD and said, "Evidence enough, Matthews?" and put it in his jacket pocket.

Matthews sat back down in his seat. "Well, well, well. I knew I couldn't trust that fucking Ortiz, raving fucking lunatic that he was. Huh. Smart little son of a bitch, though. I have to give him credit. Well, gentlemen, this does change things somewhat, doesn't it?"

Lang started to move toward him. "All right Matthews, let's go."

In that instant, Matthews reached in his desk drawer, pulled out a revolver, and pointed it at Lang. "Easy Agent, easy. Back up, back up. All right, Jake, give me the CD."

"Go fuck yourself."

"Jake, hand it over. Hand it over or I shoot Lang."

Jake looked at Mike and reached into his pocket and handed the CD to Matthews, who reached behind his desk and ran it through a shredder. "See, Jake, just like that. You lose evidence so damn easily. Well, it was nice of you boys to visit. Jake, you come here, as predicted, with this vendetta against me since I had to fire you. It's all documented in my files. Phone calls. Notes in your handwriting. Now, here you are in my office, having convinced Agent Lang here that this crazy plan was in place. I feel badly for Lang—he was stupid enough to believe you, but that's because he is your friend, I guess."

With that, Matthews took Lang's weapon. "Thank goodness Agent Lang came to my rescue. Agent, I promise you'll get a funeral with full honors for your valiant attempt at saving the life of the Attorney General of the United States. Jake, I'm afraid it's going to be worse for you. You're not just going to be a fired prosecutor, you're going to be disgraced. Your family's going to be disgraced. Committing an act against one of the chief public figures of the United States."

"Matthews, you know we played this for other people, including the President."

"So what. You can't use it against me. The original recording is gone. There's the best evidence rule and all that. It'll never hold up. They can't take me out politically. I'm a hero in this country. It's what you two don't understand. There's an enemy out there. There's a war going on. I'm the only guy fighting it, and the people know that. They want me to fight it, and they want me to win, and they're tired of all the rules and all the niceties. People like Fletcher have been selling this country down the river for years, letting people walk all over us, bending to the will of those who would destroy this country. You two think you can take me down? I'm the only person who can save this country, and I'm not going anywhere. But you two are."

And with that, he aimed Lang's Glock at Jake and fired.

CHAPTER 21

The silence was deafening. Matthews looked more puzzled than amazed. He aimed the Beretta he had taken from his desk drawer and fired at Lang, and then clicked it repeatedly, but it didn't discharge. Lang moved in, grabbed the Beretta from his hand, and retrieved his own Glock from the desk, and then put Matthews' hands behind his back.

"Benjamin Matthews, you're under arrest for the crimes set forth in the warrant, which has been served upon you. You have the right to remain silent . . ."

"I know my rights you fuck'n idiot! Let go of me! You can't prove anything! You can't touch me! You're going to pay for this, I swear to God you are going to pay for this! You have no idea what I can do to you two!"

Jake looked at Lang. "What do you think?"

Mike looked back and shrugged his shoulders. "Fuck it."

And with that, Jake hit Benjamin Matthews, Attorney General of the United States, square in the jaw as hard as he could. Matthews sunk to his knees, blood trickling from his lip. Mike yanked him to his feet.

"You'll pay for that, you bastard! You're a nothing, Jake. You've always been a nothing, and you'll always be a nothing. All you do is screw up. I'll make sure you're well taken care of."

"Matthews, you might want to consider a couple of things."

"Oh yeah, what's that?"

"One, see this?" Jake pulled a CD out of his pocket. "*This* is the disc that I played for you; this is the CD that has been in my possession since I removed the briefcase from Carlos Ortiz's vehicle on Cudjoe Key. It has been logged into evidence by the Federal Bureau of Investigation and it has remained solely in my possession from the time it was obtained until now, and it will remain in my possession or in the possession of the Department of Justice until such time as your trial. Secondly, I understand you're going to go to a party."

Matthews just looked at Jake quizzically.

"You did get an invitation from the President of the United States today, didn't you?"

Again, with that worried look in his eyes, Matthews looked at the discarded invitation on his desk. Jake reached over and picked it up. "It was nice of the President to ask you, but I think you're going to have other plans. I always liked that stamp, the one with the American Flag on it, don't you? Especially this one."

With that, Jake slowly peeled the stamp off the envelope, revealing underneath it a small black dot.

"Matthews, I'm sure you're an expert at this, but I find it amazing what they can do with recording devices these days."

Matthews stared long and hard at the envelope in Jake's hand and cast his glance at Lang. Lang merely shrugged his shoulders. "I told you to read the warrants carefully. See, in the body of that warrant is the right for us to tape our conversation with you today. Although, I have to confess, the delivery boy that brought you that invitation really wasn't one of your normal mail clerks. He did a good job, though. He made the delivery and made sure any weapons you had had no ammunition. And just to be safe, the one you knew I would have didn't have any ammunition either—but his certainly does."

And with that, Jake reached behind his back and pulled out the Beretta from his waistband.

Matthews just looked at them dumbfounded.

"One last thing Matthews. You might want to apologize to Alicia. That CD you shredded, I'm pretty sure you just destroyed a whole day's worth of her work." And for once, Benjamin Matthews had nothing to say.

CHAPTER 22

Jake spent the rest of the day at FBI Headquarters and at the Justice Department giving a video-taped deposition of what had transpired, logging the two CDs, the one from Ortiz and the one recorded in Matthews's office, and the briefcase into evidence. He waited while Mike Lang gave his videotaped statement relative to what had occurred, the finding of Ortiz's CD, the taping made at Matthews's office, and the custody of the Ortiz CD up to and including the time of its login.

It was almost 9:00 p.m. when they were finally through with everything. Fletcher had called, congratulating them and thanking them once again for their efforts on behalf of the country. Mike and Jake were sitting alone in an office and Mike sat back in his chair.

"Quite a day, buddy. Quite a day. Looks like the good guys finally won one."

"Let's hope. It's not over yet."

"Nah, it'll work out. You'll see to that."

Mike's cell phone rang and he answered. "Hold on just a minute. Jake, it's Eva. You've got to talk to her."

Jake readied himself for the tongue-lashing he was about to receive. "Hello, dear."

"Don't you 'dear' me! How dare you scare us all half to death! Jake, we thought you were dead! We didn't know what was going on. Mike couldn't tell us anything. The office is gone... all the files are gone. I don't know what to do!"

"Eva, Eva, calm down. Calm down. Everything is going to work out. I'll explain everything to you when I see you. I couldn't tell you that I was alive for your own protection. You have to believe me. There were a bunch of bad people involved in this and they had no problem with killing people."

"Jake, and poor Annie Lewis . . . that was part of this?"

"I'm afraid so. Steve and Cindy Townsend, too."

"Oh my God, no."

"Yes. So, that's why I couldn't tell you. I couldn't put you in danger. Everybody had to think I was dead until I got this thing resolved."

Eva's tone changed. "Jake, I'm so glad you're o.k. What are we going to do about the business now? Everything's gone."

"I'll take care of everything, Eva. Don't worry about it. I'll be back tomorrow or the next day and I'll explain to you what we're going to do."

"Jake, there's one more thing."

"What?"

"Jessie's back. She called. I didn't know what to tell her, so I told her you weren't available and you'd get ahold of her when you could. Jake, I didn't know what else to say."

"It's o.k., Eva. It's o.k. I'll call her. I'll talk to her."

"Jake, I tried to hide the worry in my voice, but I think she knows something's wrong."

"All right, Eva, I'll call her."

"All right, Jake. I'll talk to you then tomorrow or the next day?"

"Yes. We'll go over everything like I said and I'll take care of everything. And Eva . . ."

"Yes, Jake?"

"Again, I'm sorry. But I couldn't stand the thought of losing you, too."

There was brief silence and Jake thought he heard Eva clearing her throat. "All right, just get down here as soon as you can. We have work to do."

"Yes, ma'am. I'll see you soon."

"Well, that seemed to go pretty well," said Mike.

"You don't know Eva. I'm going to be hearing about this one for a long time."

Mike laughed to himself. "Listen, I'm going to go make sure everything is taken care of. Why don't you just stay here and call your daughter?"

"Thanks, Mike."

With that, Mike got up and opened the door.

"Mike . . ."

"Yeah?"

"I really mean thank you. Thanks for everything."

"FBI at your service, as always." And out he went.

Jake got an outside line and called Jessie.

"Daddy, what's going on? How are you?"

"I'm fine, Jessie, I'm fine."

"Daddy, the phone says the FBI is calling."

"I know, honey. I'm at FBI Headquarters in Washington, D.C."

"What's wrong?"

"There were some things that I had to help Mike Lang with. You remember Mike?"

"Sure."

"It was sort of a case we were working on together, but it's all done and everything is o.k."

"Daddy, are you sure?"

"Yeah, I'm sure. Let's talk about you, baby. How was your trip?"

"Oh, it was great. Mom and I had such a good time, Dad. I just love Rome. I can't wait to go back."

"Well, that's good. I'm glad you and your mother had fun."

"Mom talked about you a lot, Dad. I think she still misses you."

"Well, I miss her, too, and I miss you and I miss your sister."

"Yeah, I talked to Jenny, too. She's doing real well. She said she talked to you last week sometime, but she didn't know anything about what was going on, either."

"Nah, I haven't had a chance to call Jenny or your Mom. I haven't had a chance to call anybody, honey. But the case is over with and things are going to go back to normal."

"Well, as normal as we can get, right Dad?"

Jake had to laugh. Jessie had this attitude about life that was too close to his own for comfort. "That's right, honey. As close as we can."

"So, you're sure you're all right, Dad?"

"I'm fine."

"Well, I had to call. It's Monday, you know?"

"I know it is, honey. I know it is. And I can honestly tell you, everything is going to be all right."

EPILOGUE

Jake was hard at work when Eva came in. "Hey boss, you ready? It's time to go to court."

"Yeah, I'm just finishing up a couple of things here, Eva, then we'll go over."

"All right, I have everything else we need."

"Did you get in touch with Mike?"

"Yeah, he's gonna meet us there."

"O.k. I'll be out in a couple minutes."

Jake sat back and looked out the window of his new office. It was a beautiful spring day. He could hardly believe six months had passed. Per his agreement with President Fletcher, he had refused all media contacts regarding the case with Matthews, but the news media picked up enough bits and pieces to find out what had gone on and what Jake's involvement had been. He had given a two-day-long video deposition under questioning from federal prosecutors and Matthews's defense attorneys, and had received a letter from Judge Templeton, who was trying Matthews's case in the United States District Court for the Southern District, stipulating that he was excused from further trial commitments. He had convinced Mike to leave his post with the FBI and become his chief investigator, which pretty much meant his only investigator given current budget constraints. Eva had been happy to get back to work in their new office and under their new arrangement, and he had had a lot more contact with Linda and the girls. In fact, they were coming down to visit next week and he could hardly wait.

He had flown to Pennsylvania for a meeting with Linda and had apologized, as best he could, for everything that had had happened three years ago and she had accepted. They agreed to take things slow and see where things would lead, but there was hope that once again they could be a family. They knew the girls were pushing both of them, and he and Linda compared notes, laughing about their diabolical schemes for reconciliation. He had just one more thing to do to close out his past, and hopefully, get the future he wanted.

Looking at his notes one final time, he packed up his briefcase and moved to the outer office. "Eva, are you ready?"

"I'm just wait'n on you, boss. Let's go." And out they went.

It was a sunny morning and the palm trees were moving with a slight breeze as they headed to the courthouse.

"You know, Eva, I wasn't sure you'd come to the new office."

"I gave it a lot of thought. But I decided I didn't want to break in another attorney, so I had to stick with you."

Jake laughed out loud. "Compliment accepted."

They walked up the steps of the courthouse, which was packed, as Jake knew it would be, as this was going to be a pretty high-profile trial. Jake walked down the aisle, opened the gate, and took his place at the counsel table, Eva sitting beside him. The door opened and he looked around to see Mike coming in. Mike came down the aisle, patted Jake on the shoulder, and took his seat behind counsel table.

Jake looked over at the defendant and his counsel, sitting and staring impassively ahead.

"All rise," the tipstaff said, and with that everyone in the courtroom rose to their feet. Out of central casting, in strode Judge Francis Templeton, President Judge for the Southern District. White hair, glasses, and a black robe. "Please be seated," he intoned in that deep, baritone voice. "Read the caption."

The tipstaff rose. "The United States of America vs. the Defendant, Benjamin J. Matthews."

"Is the prosecution ready to proceed?"

And with that, Jake Sullivan, Chief Prosecutor for the U.S. Attorney's Miami Office, rose and said, "The United States is ready, your honor."

"And the defense?"

Winston Gates, one of Miami's premier defense lawyers rose. "Your Honor, once again we raise objections as to Mr. Sullivan prosecuting this case, he allegedly having been a participant in events that have led to a federal indictment against my client."

Judge Templeton, looking a might peeved, said, "Mr. Gates, your motion has already been overruled in previous proceedings by this court. Your raising it again doesn't do anything but irritate me. As you are aware, Mr. Sullivan gave all testimony relevant to his participation in this case via a videotaped deposition where you had a thorough right to cross-examine him, which I might add, you took advantage of for a period in excess of two days. All preliminary matters in this case, which involved testimony, statements, or activity involving Mr. Sullivan were conducted by the then Chief Prosecutor for the Miami Office of the Justice Department."

Templeton continued, "Mr. Sullivan has been reappointed Chief Prosecutor of the U.S. Attorney's Miami Office by the President of the United States and has been given a specific exemption to substitute himself for the former head prosecutor in this case. Once again, Mr. Gates, your objection is overruled. Now, are you ready to proceed?"

"We are, your Honor."

"Fine. Mr. Sullivan, you may call your first witness."

"Your Honor, I would like to call Special Investigator Michael Lang to the stand, and I would request permission from the court to play recordings of events involving the defendant, which are labeled Plaintiff's Exhibits A and B for identification."

"Mr. Sullivan, having previously listed this evidence as two of your exhibits and having filed the necessary affidavits establishing proper chain of custody, you may proceed."

With that, all the time holding Benjamin Matthews's eyes in a hard stare, Jake slowly placed the briefcase he had at his feet onto the counsel table, opened it, and removed two CDs in evidence bags labeled "A" and "B." Opening bag "A" before the court, he inserted the CD into the court's audio system and, just before pressing "play," and making sure he still had Matthews's attention, Jake Sullivan, Chief Prosecutor of the U.S. Attorney's Miami Office, grinned and winked.

WA